TONY BOWERS

ON THE NINE

ISBN: 978-0-69246-406-9

Produced in the United States of America

Vital Narrative Press
111 S. Highland Street
Memphis, TN 38111
http://vitalnarrative.com

For my loving wife Tavia,
Your love and belief in me have been invaluable

TABLE OF CONTENTS

The Genesis · 11

Something Like Baseball · 15

Peppermint & Gunpowder · 27

Batter Up · 33

Rites of Passage · 41

This Side of Glory · 57

Rip · 79

One Blood · 89

Bo Peep's Jab · 99

Gargoyles · 111

God's Precious Love · 123

Darcy's Garden · 137

ON THE NINE
BY
TONY BOWERS

THE GENESIS

Tommy lay in the darkness of his bedroom, tossing softly with his panda bear pillow, struggling to find the perfect comfortable spot to fall into a deep sleep. Outside his door the voices of his mother and father melted into the crooning of Rick James. It felt like warm honey on Tommy's ears. The sounds and movements in the living room nudged against the edges of his dark cocoon.

With a twist to the right, Tommy found that spot. Sleep fell away from Tommy as the sounds of the front room jaggedly ripped into the bedroom. There were screams and wails, grunts and the sound of crunching glass.

Tommy pushed himself out of bed. With his panda pillow cast aside, he opened the door and ran into the hall.

No, no, no!

Why you make me do that huh? Why you make me…?!

Ugh, ugh uhh!

Tommy stopped short at the rim of the room. There stood his father crying and muttering to himself.

"Why you make me?" he asked, as if each word was like taffy in his mouth. His shoulders were hunched with a jagged gin bottle remnant in his right hand. His left hand was paralyzed into a claw.

His mother sat straight like six o'clock in a ripped vinyl kitchen chair. Her face was pressed into a fright mask. Her lips were pulled low and her eyes alive with fire. She was drenched to her torso in gin and blood. Her breathing was quick and shallow. It reminded Tommy of a dying bird that had crashed against his window last summer. He watched the bird as each second pulled out into an hour, until its breathing ceased. He felt cold, wondering if history would repeat. But his mother didn't stop breathing. The middle of her scalp laid open as if it had been unzipped. The pieces of glass sparkled in her hair like diamonds in the sun.

Tommy couldn't put into words what he felt at that moment, but he did get a picture in his mind. It was of the time he was left alone on the school playground. Dusk hung heavy in the air and his mother and father weren't there to fetch him. All the other kids and adults were gone. He stared at the empty play-lot and shivered. The jungle gym looked like the skeleton of some long dead beast.

Brittle, crunchy leaves blew across the ground, sounding like a cracked baby's rattle. The metal chain of the swing knocked against the swing set pole.

Cling... chink... cling!

That vision sat in his mind as he watched his mom and dad now. He didn't know it, but the oily residue of those desolate memories would come bubbling up inside of him until the very end of his days.

SOMETHING LIKE BASEBALL

A soft September wind moved the branches of the trees back and forth. The sun was unusually hot for that time of year and beamed down on the gray concrete of the parking lot behind the school. It was a perfect Saturday for baseball.

Chris scratched the top of his head, stepped up to the batter's box and looked out at his crew with his faced screwed into a grimace. He twisted both of his ashy hands on the handle of the wooden bat as it lay on his right shoulder. He spread his legs and bent his knees as he got into his stance. His best friend Ben was hunched over with one eye closed with the other staring right at the batter's box spray painted on the wall of the school. He stood up straight, squeezed the orange rubber ball and went into his pitcher's stretch. His throwing arm went up high over his head, and like a propeller on a plane, came down so fast it was a blur. Chris narrowed his eyes as the orange ball whizzed toward him. Head down, eyes open, he twisted his

15

body and swung the bat over the top of the ball.

"Strike 2!" Eli called from the field.

The ball hit the wall and bounced back to Ben who had a huge grin on his face. The rest of the crew laughed at Chris' exaggerated motions. He flopped over from the swing and had to straighten himself out. Tank stood in an area were first base would be. He shook his shiny head and waved both hands at Chris.

"Whew boy! You blew me down with all that wind!" he cackled.

Eli was lined up at second and he strutted back and forth clapping his hands. "One more! One more! Strike him out so we can go!"

Phil was way out at the edge of the lot in what they considered the outfield. He started to do jumping jacks and called out, "Hey batter, batter!"

Strikeout was a game inner city kids invented because there were no 'diamonds in the rough.' So, wherever there was a brick wall, kids spray painted a square with an X in the middle to serve as the target the pitcher aimed for. They played with a rubber ball or sometimes a tennis ball. The pitcher would rear back and let it fly with all his might. If the pitcher could place the ball inside the box or on the X as the batter swung and missed, it was ruled a strike. If a kid in the "field" caught the ball in two bounces or less, then it was their turn to bat.

Ben hunched over once again getting ready to let the ball fly. He stared at the strikeout box like there was an imaginary catcher kneeling down giving signals. One finger meant fastball. Ben shook off the imaginary sign. Two fingers, curve ball, another shake off.

Chris blew air from his mouth in mild disgust because there was only one pitch Ben was going to throw and that was a fastball.

Chris got in his stance and settled himself. He thought about his grandfather's instructions on batting.

Head still, eyes open, swing through the ball.

It was his Grand-Pop George that introduced him to the game when he was a real little shorty. Chris loved the game. Grand-Pop George would sit with him and explain the rules when the Cubs came on WGN.

"See that Chrissie?" he would say. "The right fielder has got to be able to hit the cut-off man. If not, he ain't worth a quarter."

Chris hung on Grand-Pop's every word. Chris' father hated the Cubs and wanted his son to be a White Sox fan.

"It don't make no sense for a South Side boy to be no uppity, North Side Cubs fan. It ain't right."

"Junior, you talking crazy. Ain't nothing wrong with this boy being no Cubs fan. Besides the Sox don't come on TV as much. You love what you see on the regular."

Chris' father would just wave his hand and stomp out of the room. Chris and Grand-Pop would giggle and then go back to Larry Bowa turning a double play to Leon Durham.

This was a special day for the crew. Both

Chicago teams were in contention. Back in the day it was one or the other, but having both teams? It was almost too good to be true. In all twelve years of his life, neither team had been this good, this late in the season. To top it off, both of their games were on TV.

The Cubs were going against the Padres at 1:20 p.m. and the White Sox game started at 3:00 p.m. The crew couldn't believe their luck. Ben had an idea that they would watch both games at the same time at his house. Two games at the same time! It was 1986, years before picture-in-picture. The plan was to watch the Cubs game on the floor model color TV and then when the Sox game came on, they would bring down Ben's black and white TV from his room and set it on top of the floor model. It was baseball paradise for the crew.

Chris was ready. Ben spun his arm like a windmill and stared icy daggers at Chris. Then he stopped in mid motion.

Chris frowned and yelled. "Is this some new pitch you working on fool? Just let it go!"

"I would, but your boy is in the way."

Chris looked around and saw Fats wobbling toward him. He was the neighborhood hustle man and even though it was only one in the afternoon, he was drunk as two skunks. When it came to hustle men, Fats wasn't a very good one. He never had anything anybody ever wanted. Things like 8-track players, when the Sony Walkman was the new thing. He would try to sell old school Chuck Taylor Converse when everyone was rocking Adidas. It seemed like Fats was always two steps behind. So mostly he stayed drunk and wandered through the hood to pass the time.

Fats stood next to Chris who pushed his top lip against his nose to block the smell.

"What you want?" Eli screamed. "We got a game going on."

Fats leaned back as if the words themselves pushed him away. "Ahh, let me get a swing."

"A swig? Fool, we don't drink, we just kids!" Chris said.

"Naw, little man. I want to swing the bat."

"Don't give it to him, Chris. We gotta get home to watch the game.

Fats swayed from foot to foot and moved his lips back and forth like he was rubbing in Chap Stick. "I used to play ball back in the day. Let me swing."

"Used to play ball? Right!" Ben laughed. "What was the name of your team? The Burbank Bums?"

"Right, go sell some squares," Eli laughed.

Fats looked at Chris with his bloodshot eyes. "Come on! I won't even need a ball," he pleaded. Chris' ears shot up.

"How you gonna do that?" Ben asked with a laugh. "Magic?"

Chris shrugged and against the wishes of his crew, he handed Fats the bat.

"Ah man!"

"What you do that for?"

"Now we gonna miss the start of the game!"

Chris shushed the crew. "It's cool. I want to see

how he handles it. Just one swing, right?"

"See, a kid with some respect," Fats said with a smile. "Look here kid. Let me show you how they taught me in the Pony Leagues. This all-star stuff here. Watch me. Keep the bat at two o'clock and keep your hips tight. That's how Ryno does it."

Chris' ears perked up again. Ryne Sandberg was his favorite player. It was something about him. The way he fielded and swung was so controlled yet powerful. Chris wanted to be just like him.

Fats gripped the bat and shimmied his hips like a dancer enticing a lover. Chris watched him like a great secret was being revealed.

"And when the pitch comes in the right spot you turn your hips, drop your elbow a bit and let it go. Just let it go," Fats said as he followed through with the swing. Chris stared at him like he was fresh off the back page of the Sun-Times. Damn if he didn't look like Sandberg.

"He did play," Chris mumbled. He knew only a real ball player could put all the mechanics together just right to produce such a beautiful swing. And as if it was a real game, Chris followed the invisible ball up into an endless blue sky. The others stared at Fats and nobody said a word. Chris was struck by how blue the sky was that day. He had only seen a sky as blue and massive like that once before.

It was two years ago and his Grand-Pop took him and a few cousins to Wrigley Field. It was his first time. They had to take two buses and a train to get there. It felt like a journey to a magical kingdom. As they marched through the intersection of Clark and Addison, the excitement danced across Chris' arm causing small goose pimples to rise like braille across his skin.

"This way, boys."

Chris and the others followed behind Grand-Pop as his long legs covered enough steps to make up three of theirs. On the journey to get there, Grand-Pop had told the boys of the days when black men weren't allowed into Wrigley.

"Hell, you couldn't even be on that side of town unless you were a domestic working in some white person's house," he started. "Other folk worked and died to make it possible for us to simply go to a ball game. So it's really more than just baseball." Chris would stare at Grand-Pop whenever he would talk about the past. It was like he was looking into a portal that had opened up in front of him. The grayish-blue that surrounded his brown irises seemed to glow and his shoulders got square and stiff.

The inside of Wrigley felt like an old Catholic church with its high stone ceilings and the way the echoes of the people reverberated and filled the space so that it sounded like a million people spoke all at once.

Grand-Pop turned and handed each of them a torn ticket stub and then climbed the flight of stairs. Chris was bringing up the rear. Grand-Pop stood surveying a great vista of seats in the stadium grandstand.

"This way," Grand-Pop pointed. They marched down past the rows of green wooden seats. The grandstand was covered in the shadows of the upper deck but further down to the edge, the sun cut across the seats like a lemon wedge.

"Are we down there, Pop? That far down?"

"Just come on."

Chris could barely control himself. The field was coming more into view. The deep and chilly shade gave way to the bright and warm July sun.

"This is us." Grand-Pop pointed to an empty set of seats five rows back from the first baseline. Chris slapped five with his cousins and did a duck dance before stepping into the row.

"Boy, you know you silly," Grand-Pop laughed. "I'll get us some popcorn when the man comes by. Well boys, this here is Wrigley Field. What you think?"

His two cousins chattered like excited squirrels while Chris sat in silence. The field was the deepest green he had ever laid eyes on. It reminded him of an emerald he had seen in an encyclopedia at school. The thick ivy that grew from the wall blew slowly in the summer breeze. Chris imagined the secrets that could be held behind the wall as if the ivy gave way to another world beyond this one. Crews of men, of all shapes and colors, raked at the infield dirt. There was a spirit that settled around him. It was rich and thick and felt like a hug. Chris looked up and saw the sky.

"Grand-Pop," he asked, pausing briefly. "Is the sky different over here?"

Grand-Pop chuckled. "Naw, Chris. It's the same sky and sun."

"But I've never seen it so... so blue before."

"Son, that's the excitement of a ball game. Everything seems brighter and better."

"Then I want to spend the rest of my life playing ball then."

"Ha! I understand, Chris. Popcorn's here!" Grand-Pop lifted his hand to hail the vendor who skipped over to their row, ready to dish out the buttery goodness. Chris was caught up in the cerulean vista until the Cubs and the Astros took the field.

"I'm not trying to miss the first pitch!" Ben yelled, bringing Chris back to the present. He shook free from the magic sky and looked back at the reality of the broken concrete. The crew began to gather their things. Chris looked at Fats, who leaned to his right with the bat resting on his shoulder.

"Where'd you play ball?" Chris asked.

"Right here at Hirsch," Fats answered. "We had the best teams back in the day. In '73, Rickey Green took us to the state championship in basketball and we won city that year in baseball. I was batting cleanup. We was the shit. And I could really swing it. Ryno stole my style. Can you believe that?" Fats gave the bat back to Chris who looked at it as if it was made of gold.

Tank walked over to Chris as Fats turned and

stumbled up the street and out of sight.

"Let's get out of here. The game is starting."

"That was tight, wasn't it?"

"Yeah, it was a good swing, but so what?"

"What you mean 'so what'! That looked just like Sandberg, man."

"Yeah, well it ain't. Sandberg is at Wrigley, getting ready to get paid for swinging the bat. That fool gonna go throw up behind the dumpster in the alley."

Chris' face balled up as a lump formed in his throat. "That's mean, man," he said.

"That fool did it to himself," he said with a wave of the hand. "Ain't nobody tell him to jack his life up like that."

Chris was silent.

"You cool, fool?" Ben asked.

"Yeah. What time is it?"

"Time for you to get a watch," Phil said, as he jokingly pushed Chris in the back of his head.

They cut through the green fields of Grand Crossing Park toward Ben's house on Greenwood. They laughed and made predictions on the games. Eli almost choked at the possibility that the Cubs and Sox could meet in the World Series. Chris shook his head as his sadness evaporated a bit. He understood at that moment that baseball could be like life, full of possibilities and hope. The lump Chris felt earlier was for Fats. He felt sorry for him.

There was magic in baseball. Chris could feel it

creep over his skin as he watched a game. The goose bumps and raised hair were evidence. In baseball, just like life, you got a chance to get your cuts in and sometimes a hit would be the result. And sometimes, you struck out. But with a short memory, you could enjoy having played the game and rest well in the fact that you were going to have a chance to go at it again. There is always another game tomorrow.

But somehow, some way, baseball season was coming to an end for Fats. Chris could feel it in his bones. The enemy of baseball is the crisp winds of winter. Chris felt a slight chill when Fats walked away. It was as if Fats' own personal winter was at hand.

PEPPERMINT & GUNPOWDER

The radiator hissed like a mad cobra. The intensity of the heat was muted slightly by the tentative January breeze that tripped over the windowsill. Tommy inhaled deeply, taking in the flowery smell of Tide from the sheets of his bed. He was glad to be off the cold closet floor. He and his mother sat there watching Dick Clark's Rocking New Year's Celebration on the 12-inch black and white. It was 1983 and the hood was alive with gunfire. Shots had fired on New Year's Eve every year of Tommy's decade of life. He imagined that it would always be the case, even when he had children of his own. He saw himself as a grown man sitting with them in the bottom of a closet, watching a century year old Clark gush about the latest pop tunes. Tommy enjoyed the looseness and the quiet of those moments when his father was absent. He and his mother never talked about things that had happened, but the moistness in her eyes said plenty. As he slept, an ambulance streaked up 79th Street, a half block up from their apartment. Tommy didn't flinch at the wailing siren, but his eyes sprung open as an avalanche of footfalls roared toward the door. A key hit the lock and his blood ran cold.

"Shut the hell up! Making all that damn noise and shit!" said a voice from the front of his house.

It was his father. Tommy learned at a young age that he was never to refer to his father by anything other than his street name. Instead of Dad, he was only known as Brick.

Brick's baritone shook the apartment. And the other voices were from his crew, Rob and Rush, collectively known as the Drunk Brothers.

"Ah man, who sleep anyway?" Rob asked. "It's New Year's! Everybody supposed to be partying anyhow."

Tommy silently rolled over and faced the wall of his room. He prayed that morning would come sooner than usual and that no drama would pop off. But as the music started and the laughter swelled, he knew what was up. Tommy lay in bed, watching the ceiling as if it were a movie screen as he listened to Brick bully the Drunk Brothers. Tommy glanced at the red embers of his digital clock.

3:37 a.m.

They had been partying for an hour and there seemed to be no slowing up. Tommy tried to strain against the sounds to hear the squeak of his mother's door. Would she engage? Was she praying for peace like him? Just then, the voices of the men got big and sharp. Curses, threats and boasts were the usual script when there was too much alcohol and pride mixed together.

Suddenly, Tommy's door swung open and the broad-shouldered shadow of his father filled the doorway. Tommy swallowed hard.

"Tommy, wake up!" he bellowed. "You gotta help me get this money!" Tommy rolled his eyes and bit the inside of his cheek.

Before he knew exactly what was going on, Tommy was standing on the back porch of their apartment, gripping a pistol. He held the gun loosely as he aimed it at the alley below.

"Hold the damn gun right!" Brick snapped. "Don't make me look bad."

The Drunk Brothers let out a collective cackle.

"No way he gonna hit that can!" Rush let out. "That's like a hundred feet away!"

"G-g-gon'…buy me a…fifth of Crown Royal with my part of…of this money," Rob slurred.

Brick bet the brothers that Tommy could drink four shots of liquor and hit a trashcan from the back porch with his twenty-two automatic. Fifty dollars was on the line which was the same as a day's pay. Brick folded his massive arms and told Tommy what was at stake.

The Drunk Brothers didn't say what type of liquor he could have, so Brick poured four shots of peppermint schnapps, lined up in a row on the porch railing.

Once they realized what was going on, they began to protest. "Aw man, a little girl could drink a whole bottle of schnapps!" Rush pleaded. But Brick cussed them out until they gave in.

Tommy's hand hung over the first glass. He turned and looked back into the apartment. Tommy imagined his mother was hiding behind her bedroom door, too afraid to do anything. When she didn't appear, Tommy took each shot straight to the head. It didn't burn his throat much.

"Now steady yourself," Brick said. "Squeeze the trigger and hit that can." There were tornados in Brick's eyes. Tommy had seen the gun in action a few times and those same tornados whirled. The twenty-two once caught a kid who'd cheated at craps in the thigh. He was only a few years older than Tommy, maybe even in high school.

Tommy was afraid of the pistol. But he was afraid of his father more. Brick sucked his front teeth and Tommy tightened his grip on the handle.

The only light in the alley was right over the trashcan. It was bathed in yellow like an exhibit in a museum. Tommy closed his left eye and concentrated. The babblings of the Drunk Brothers fell away and echoed like Tommy had descended into a cave. He licked his lips and tasted the slick residue of the schnapps. He pulled the trigger.

Pop!

The shot tore through the night sky as the gun

tried to jump out of Tommy's hand. The bullet hit the can dead center and the Drunk Brothers rolled over in disgust.

"Now pay me my money!" Brick bellowed. They handed him lumps of bills and cussed bitterly.

"I guess that boy of yours ain't such a poindexter after all," Rob said.

"Yeah," Rush chimed in ."Guess you gonna start claiming him to the fellas down at the pool hall." The brothers howled.

Brick shook his head and smiled as he counted the money. Tommy stood there waiting for a high five or for Brick to say, 'that was good, boy.' But there was nothing. He just went on counting the cash.

Tommy felt a rush of hot air. His skin smoldered like the bottom of a steam iron left on too long. He squeezed the trigger and lit up the air. When a bullet hit the trashcan, it jumped, flipped and danced like the tail of a kite in a stiff wind. Bullets struck the ground, the light post and the Johnson's garage. Tommy kept squeezing until the gun went silent.

The weight of Brick's hand lowered the gun slightly. He slid the pistol from Tommy's grip and grabbed his shoulder. Brick's lips moved but Tommy couldn't hear him. The gun smoke hung in the air like a curtain. The brothers coughed and Tommy's eyes were beginning to burn. They stared like Tommy was the drunk one. Rob flapped his arms wildly and spit out some words. Tommy looked down at the alley. The Johnson's lights burst on. Several other houses followed. Brick shoved Tommy inside. The Drunk Brothers tripped out the front door. Brick pointed to Tommy's bedroom. He floated into the room and closed the door. Tommy had never experienced such power before. He was noticed and regarded.

He lay in his bed, head throbbing, and still feeling the weight of the gun inside his hand. Tommy finally drifted off to sleep as the sun rose, with the sweetness of peppermint schnapps on his lips and the taste of gunpowder in his throat.

BATTER UP

Tank flexed his fingers on the smooth blond wood of the bat and got a vision of the emerald green field of Wrigley. He could smell the fresh cut grass mixed with peanuts and warm beer. He could feel a gentle breeze that moved the ivy on the wall like a wave on Lake Michigan.

Even on his black and white, Cubs' baseball was something to behold. It didn't matter if it were Larry Bowa or Shawon Dunston at shortstop, there was going to be magic as the ball rolled across the bronze-colored dirt and into a spit-stained glove.

He wanted to be there now, to feel the slight cramp in his lower back from sitting in the bleachers for four hours. Wrigley was like Shangri-La, Mecca or Lady Liberty. It was more than bricks and mortar, even more than baseball.

The first time he walked down the stairs of the grandstand and saw the field, he felt a connection to all who had been there before him. The bricks, the ivy, the scoreboard and every blade of grass brought him into something bigger than just a game. It transcended everything except the gulf that was between him and his father.

"Wanna watch the game, Rip?"

"Ugh," he answered in disgust. Rip never had any notion about baseball. Tank felt the disappointment coming from his father because there were no street hustle games that he wanted to learn. Tank preferred a bat and a ball, and at times, just a simple book. Whatever magic baseball bestowed on him, Tank knew the blood of a dead man would soon wash it all away.

"On three, we gonna bust this fucker open like a rotten tomato," Rip whispered.

Tank looked down at the man sleeping like a tit-fed baby, completely unaware that his head was about to split like a cabbage.

Tank's heart shot into his throat and he struggled to speak. "W-w-why?" he stammered out.

"Fucker stole three hundred dollars out my pocket."

"Who is this?"

"Do it matter?"

Tank batted his eyelids, "Well, yeah. It's wrong to beat somebody, you know… I guess?"

Rip lowered his own bat, rolled his head to the left and hissed. "It's the ones you know that'll screw you over the hardest!"

Tank stopped listening. Rip's voice fell away as

if he was descending into a deep underground vault.

It had been the Friday night dominoes game that birthed this strife. It was always a rough time when they played, but Tank remembered that the voices were sharper and the tension hotter than any time before. He put his head under his pillows to try and block it all out. He finally made it to sleep somehow.

Tank came out from beneath the blanket of his thoughts. Fats? He thought to himself, beginning to recognize the man as he slept.

"I was nice enough to let the nigger sleep on the recliner," Rip grunted. "Up here crying about his momma putting him out. I should have left his ass on the street. He fucked up the game anyhow, with all that bitching and moaning. I'm going to enjoy this."

"Wait. How you know you didn't lose the money?" Tank asked.

"You think I would lose track of three hundred dollars? I know I had it last night and he was the only nigger left. Who else could it be?" he asked with a snarl. "Now…on three, you swing low…I got him high."

Tank's mind spun like bicycle wheels on summer days as he clasped his eyes shut.

"One," Rip started. Tank couldn't catch his breath and his stomach bubbled.

"Two," Rip continued. Tank opened his eyes as Rip balanced the bat inches over Fats' face, who was now smiling in his ignorant slumber. Tank wondered what he was dreaming about and hoped it was a good one because it would be his last.

"Three!" Rip's bat seemed to fall in slow motion. Calmly, Tank jabbed his bat and blocked Rip's swing.

Clack!

The bats clashed, forming a perfect X. Fats' eyes shot open like they were on springs. It took a second for the confusion to fall from his gaze. He looked up and saw Rip and Tank frozen, bats crossed high like two combatants dueling at dawn.

"What the fuck?!" Fats jumped from the recliner and ran for the door. Rip swept his leg and Fats tumbled and rolled. Rip threw his bat and clipped Fats' head. Unfazed, he hacked at the door lock until it opened. Rip took off after him. Tank dropped his bat, leapt and draped himself over Rip's shoulders, bringing him to his knees. Once Fats had cleared the door, Tank jumped up and stepped back panting.

Rip stayed down on one knee with his head craned toward the door. His fingers clenched the thick strands of the shag carpet.

"You out of your mind?" he asked as he slowly rose to his feet. "I'm gonna take that three hundred out of your ass!"

Tank withered. "I know you mad. But I couldn't let you," he whispered.

"Couldn't? I'm your daddy. You follow me!" Rip screamed as he stomped across the floor until he was nose to nose with Tank. He gripped him by the collar. "Why?" he demanded.

Tank's eyes fluttered like butterflies eluding the hands of a child. "Cause…we can get more money, but…dead is dead."

Rip pursed his lips into a tight line. "You ain't like me. You might as well be a damn orphan as different as you are from me," Rip whispered.

Tank felt a jab to his gut and he fought back tears. Then, suddenly, a violent shift happened inside of his chest near his heart. It reminded him of a nature program he had seen on PBS. It was an avalanche on a frost-capped mountain. A massive shelf of ice and snow slid, broke and tumbled swiftly down the side of the mountain. What was cold, white and gray was now gone, leaving behind green and brown matted grass, mud and stone. The mountain was uncovered and strong in its glory.

Tank couldn't help but smile as the tears rolled down. Rip flinched.

"What the hell is going on around here?" a female's voice interjected.

Tank looked over Rip's shoulder toward the front door. "Mommy," he whispered.

"Rip, what's happening? That fool Fats ran me down getting outta here. Somebody say something!"

"Fats stole from us," Rip said without looking at her. "I was about to tune him up when your son stopped me."

She set down the grocery bags "Stole what?"

"Three hundred."

"Rip…I took the money," she said.

Rip spun around. "What? Why you going in my pockets?"

"You were too drunk. I couldn't wake you up to get the grocery money…Jesus!" She shook her head and covered her mouth. Tank thought he saw new wrinkles appear on his mother's face. He loved looking at pictures of her when she was younger. She was so carefree. He wished he had known her back in the day. Now she seemed tired all the time and she moved slowly even though she wasn't even thirty yet.

"I can't take any more of this. You gotta stop the drinking and the drugging. It's made you crazy. You going to beat a man to death over some money and have your son help you?"

"Look, don't start that bullshit now—" he interjected.

"No!" she bellowed. "Now whatever you do to yourself, whatever you do to me is one thing. But you leave him the hell out of this!"

"We all in this shit together," Rip hissed. " Just one big happy family." He turned and shuffled to the bedroom.

Tank looked at his mother who didn't meet his eyes. She picked up the bags and went into the kitchen. Tank stood alone in the living room. The crinkling of plastic grocery bags coming from the kitchen was the only sound in the apartment. He knew that was the end of it. They would never speak of this again.

He galloped down the front stairs to get the rest of the groceries. He glanced at his watch. It was only two more hours until the Cubs game.

RITES OF PASSAGE

I

Richard walked out of school with the orange and mellowed sun melted on top of the pale gray sky as his backdrop. His head bowed, he looked at the tops of his black tassel dress shoes. The sound of crunching gravel in the parking lot marked the end of a long day of teaching.

Ha, ha!

Shit!

He looked up and saw three lean figures posted against the schoolyard fence. He recognized one of his students named Rashard with two neighborhood thugs who had graduated a few years back.

Richard shook his head. "How come you didn't come to class, young blood?"

"I was at the studio," Rashard answered. "I ain't miss nothing no way."

"Yeah that's what you think. You can't be a rap mogul and a seventh grade drop out, Rashard. You gotta get your education too. You can do both."

The boy lowered his head and giggled. The neighborhood referred to him as Rashard the Legend and Richard liked him. He was smart and had a keen sense of the world. He would smile broadly and shake his head whenever he sniffed bullshit. And most things in life were bullshit to him. Richard thought it was sad for someone so young to be so cynical, but he tried not to judge too much. He understood that life on The Nine wasn't easy.

"I gotta get this in, Mr. T. I mean, I'm about to blow up. These streets be begging for this here." He waved his hands over his body as if he was a product on display.

"There's time, Rashard. You just gotta slow down."

"I can't. I gotta blaze this here. I don't know when my time is gonna come. You know how it is. You from around here. I gotta get my piece of the pie now."

"But if you make some changes son, you can have the whole pie. You get me?"

One of the lean thugs scoffed. The other looked at Richard as if he had three heads. Things weren't so different from when Richard roamed the Grand Crossing neighborhood as a young turk. You had to be aware and careful because the streets knew no mercy. But what was different was that life seemed to be stuck in fast-forward for this generation. Kids grew up quickly and were hurtled toward an uncertainty that slammed the door on their childhood.

Rashard chuckled. "That's a good one, Mr. T. You always keep it real. Look, I'm in class for the rest of the marking period. I promise."

"The rest of the marking period? It's only two weeks until the end of the year, boy."

Rashard shrugged and gave that smile that enraptured everyone who saw it. Richard clasped hands with him and pulled him into a hug. As they parted, Richard saw a current of electricity in Rashard's eyes and his smile was like the hope a new day brings when the sun peeks over the horizon. Richard drove away from the school feeling satisfied that he knew that all his children were okay.

Rashard was the only absent student that day. When he didn't show by ten a.m., Richard began to worry. He plowed on with the lessons on pre-algebra and dividing unlike fractions.

Richard drove with no music. He crossed the invisible barrier of 79th Street when he veered onto the Dan Ryan Expressway. He headed due north toward Hyde Park. It seemed to him that the sky was a shade lighter as he got further from Grand Crossing. The stars shined a tad brighter. Growing up on 81st and Evans was easier in the eighties. But through the passage of time, the neighborhood shifted and things got darker for the incoming generations. Even the days of crack couldn't compare to what the youngsters of Rashard's generation had to deal with.

As Richard pulled into the driveway of his gray

stone, two-story flat, his wife's red Lexus was already there. He felt a calm come over him that eased his shoulders down a bit. He walked into the apartment and Neo-soul filled the air. Rhonda hummed to Maxwell and the rest of Richard's stress was washed away.

"Hey suga," he called out.

"Richard!" she said excitedly, prancing into the front room to greet him. She had changed from the gray business suit to a flowing rayon red and blue wrap. Her jet-black pixie cut was as fresh as the day she came home from the stylist a week ago. Her smile was bright and cheerful. His heart ballooned. Her arms were spread wide and he took her in his own. He hugged her and sniffed her neck and sweet jasmine filled his nostrils. Her shapely body pressed perfectly against him. He caressed her back as he kissed the side of her honey colored neck. He let his hands come to rest on the apex of her round derriere.

"How was your day, my love?" she asked, gazing up into his eyes.

"Not great. The best part was the drive home. But it's all good now." He leaned down and kissed her again, sucking on her plump, sweet bottom lip.

"Ooh," she said coyly. "You trying to get it in before dinner, huh?"

"Before and after."

"It must have been a tough day."

"Yeah. I just wonder if I'm making a difference with these kids."

Rhonda furrowed her brow slightly and pursed her lips. "You are. Just by being there...you are."

"Being there doesn't seem like enough. I want to see their lives moving in a better direction."

She ran her hand across his shoulder blades in an attempt to relax him. "Rich, you spend six hours a day with those kids. They have to go home and live in the stuff that's throwing everything out of whack. It's only so much you can do. You gotta know that, love."

He sniffed and smiled. He looked deeply in her eyes and knew she was right. Since he had left the corporate world and gotten into education, he carried the weight of an entire generation on his shoulders. He thought back to that day three years ago when he sat at his office desk at Taylor, Forte & Mason, one of the leading accounting firms in the city. He looked down on Michigan Avenue. Twenty stories below, the people looked like ants pushing against one another and he felt a deep tug on his soul. He had just read about a huge riot at Crane High School on the West Side. The Sun-Times had it splashed on the front page. Still pictures of mayhem and chaos and black lives tossed and turned inside out.

He wanted to make a difference and felt that being a teacher was the way. For him, seventh grade was a key year. Each black boy and girl faced a crossroads in his or her lives at that age.

He wanted to be a director that pointed them to a path that lead them past the horizon where they could blossom and spring up full of color and life—a place where they didn't have to deal with the weeds of their surroundings.

Rhonda was so supportive when he told her of his plan. She didn't even flinch when he told her his salary would drop by twenty grand. He didn't think it possible before then, but he fell deeper in love with her that day.

After dinner they made love, softly and slowly. He wanted to feel every inch of her. After nine years of marriage, he never grew tired of feeling her every curve. Her plush and supple angles cascading over his hard and rigid straight lines were still a highlight for him.

The light of the moon rimmed the edges of the curtains in the dark bedroom. Rhonda slept soundly on his chest. The heaviness of her body made him proud. He was her support.

He stared up to the dark ceiling and wondered about his mission. The drain of being a surrogate father to eighty-five preteens was affecting him. He lied to himself about that. Not wanting to admit the truth that laid inside of his heart. He wondered if Rhonda would be disappointed if he quit.

Beep!

A text had just come through on his phone. He turned to the nightstand on his side of the bed and the pale green light from the phone illuminated the room. He reached over gently as not to disturb Rhonda. He thumbed the buttons of the phone and retrieved the text. The light from the phone cast his face in a ghostly shade as he read the message from his principal.

Give me a call. One of ours has been shot.

His chest ceased up and he rose. Rhonda flopped over and fell out of her sleep.

"What's up?"

"Uh, I'm sorry sweetie. I, uh...Mrs. Adkins just sent me a text. A student's been shot." He got up from the bed and hit the call button. Mrs. Adkins voice jumped on the line and confirmed his fear.

Rhonda sat up in bed and switched on the lamp on the nightstand on her side. Concern was heavy on her face as she watched Richard pace back and forth. The phone was pressed against his ear as he listened intently.

"Ok. I'm on my way."

Richard put his phone down and looked toward Rhonda as she hugged her knees. He began to put on a pair of jeans. He spoke and dressed.

"It's Rashard," he said with a heavy sigh. "He was hanging out on 79th and...somebody...they don't know who...they drove up and started shooting. He got caught up. He's at Stroger. Damn, U of C. They should have a trauma center. He should be there, its closer," he mumbled to himself. Rhonda scooted to the foot of the bed and began to dress. "Oh babe, you don't have to come. You got work in the morning."

"Rich, stop," she said with a serious, but loving glance. "I'm going with you." He sighed gratefully.

They drove toward the hospital along the Dan Ryan. The moon was high and full as the quiet storm on the radio played softly, filling in the gaps of their silence.

The muted bleach and chalk smell of the hospital greeted them as they walked into the emergency room. He saw Mrs. Adkins and a crowd he assumed to be family huddled in the waiting room. He walked hand in hand with Rhonda and joined the group. Their cries, inquiries and sobs joined together like a collective wail of pain. Just off to the left was Rashard's mother. She was hunched over and her knees were bent. An older woman, who Richard assumed was her mother, attempted to hold her up. Fresh rivers flowed down her round cheeks. Her lips quivered as she let out a soft moan. Richard's heart skipped and jumped against his rib cage. He squeezed Rhonda's hand and she pressed against his side. He heard Rhonda sniff as her own tears flowed. Mrs. Adkins looked at him but did not speak.

Just then a chill floated through the air. Like someone had opened a window during a windstorm. Richard felt the hair on the back of his neck stand up.

"Jesus!" the older woman holding up Rashard's mother called. "Jesus!" she let out again, over and over hoping it would calm the pain in her spirit.

Suddenly, the air got colder and filled the room. Rhonda began to shiver and as quickly as the chill had arrived, it was gone in the same instant. The temperature became normal and the hair on her neck laid down again.

Rashard's mother's eyes grew large and her

pupils drew in. Her lips pulled back into a silent scream. Then after a second or two she began to howl. She fell back and a young man supported the older woman and kept Rashard's mother from crashing to the ground. Like an initial domino, her screams set off a chain reaction and the entire waiting room was lit with wails of grief. Richard's chest heaved quickly and his knees got week. He threw his arm around Rhonda and hugged her tightly. Mrs. Adkins shook her head as she looked toward the floor. She two-stepped back and forth in a small imaginary box, her black coily hair and ample bosom bounced up and down as she spoke in a garbled and ancient tongue. The unknown words passed overhead like a dove with wings spread over the room. Other voices picked up the foreign tongue and their voices were unified. Richard felt a peace settle over him like a gentle mist. The wails lessened a bit. They had placed Rashard's mother in a chair and fanned her with a folded newspaper. The doctor, short and brown with sorrow filled eyes stepped into the room and gave the news that everyone already knew.

II

On the day of the funeral, the sun was angry. Its burning glare caused Richard to chink up his eyes. He put his hand to his forehead like a soldier's salute to block the searing rays. Coming out of the dim funeral parlor made it hard for his eyes to adjust. Eventually Al's Italian Beef across the street from the funeral parlor came into focus. The smell of grilled onions and fried polish sausages were so heavy that he could taste the grease.

The Howard Funeral Parlor was perfectly situated on Cottage Grove near 79th Street. It was the chosen place to lay to rest all the lives lost on the Southeast side of Chicago. Richard remembered seeing his first dead body while peering in a window of the parlor. He and his friends were coming from the McDonalds located on 77th and Cottage. A round-faced kid named Ben had dared Richard to take a look. Never being one to back down from a dare, Richard stood on a stone planter and peered inside. He saw a pearl white casket holding a dusty brown man in rest. He looked as if he was, maybe in his thirties. He was dressed in a black suit with gold pinstripes. He peacefully laid with his arms folded over his chest.

There were no mourners. He just rested in a hall, as if it was waiting his turn on stage. Richard's heart ached for the lonely body. No one was there to cry. He dropped tears and turned from the window. He quickly wiped them away. He won the dare and gained a lesson that day.

The funeral organ mixed with the honking, wheezing traffic of 79th Street filled with cars, buses and hustle men as activity on The Nine rarely ever stopped. Life or death, it beat on ceaselessly—the mixture of sounds like dozens of cats in heat dancing with asthmatic cows.

Chicago simmered. It was as if someone held the lid on a pot, pushing down the rising steam. The weight of the other mourners pressed against Richard like an aggressive hug. He stopped in his tracks and sighed. Even though they had all come together to say goodbye to Rashard, there was a divide the size of a canyon between him and the man he sat next to inside the funeral parlor. Each man, woman and child sat on his or her own island of grief.

"How you doing, babe?" Rhonda asked.

He looked down on his wife, sighed and squeezed her hand. "I'm...ok. You know... this hurts... it just really hurts, sweetie."

"I know."

He nodded his head and thought how Rashard represented all of his students with their unbridled potential and energy. He knew that if that energy was harnessed correctly, it could push them all into another galaxy. Rashard was their visionary, their shaman. He was their bridge between the grand creator and the physical world. Their voice was now silenced, leaving behind frustration and crushed dreams.

"Want to get something to eat?" she asked.

"Yeah. Want to meet up at Cooper's Hawk? I need some wine."

"Sounds divine, love. I got a taste for that barrel reserve red."

"Two glasses for me."

He leaned down and kissed her lips. She floated away from him. They decided to drive separately because Rhonda needed to run to her office before the funeral began. She stopped to hug Rashard's mother.

She held her close and whispered in her ear. The two women shared words spoken softly and gently. After a few moments, she released her embrace and Rashard's mother waved goodbye as Rhonda proceeded up the street.

The mourners began to splinter off and Richard stood looking as the pallbearers slide the glossy dark wooden casket trimmed in gold into the back of the white hearse. There were still wet eyes surrounding him, but the conversations started to sound normal again.

You going to the repast?
Yeah.
They gonna have drinks?
I gotta pick up my baby, but I'll see you.
I gotta go to work.
Life was already moving on.

Richard had already given his condolences to Rashard's mother. Two male family members guided her into the back of the limo. The heavy car door slammed. The engine erupted and then settled into a steady hum.

Boom-bap! Boom! Boom! Bap!
Richard turned towards the sound of the drums. They came from a vacant lot next to the Al's Italian Beef. A congregation of youngsters had gathered. The crowd of teens juked and jived to what Richard recognized as Rashard's coming out song.

Pocket Town Run It.
The crowd sang out in unison. Richard

overheard a young girl saying before the funeral that she was there the night Rashard was shot.

"On everything I love, I swear I heard the Legend's voice rapping after he got shot."

Richard thought about that during the service. How he felt Rashard's soul pass over him at the hospital. The weight of it all creased Richard's face, the mortal becoming immortal. Rashard was gone in physical form, but his voice and message would live on.

All day, we be on the block all day...

Echoing against the gray concrete apartment buildings of the Grand Crossing/Chatham/Park Manor neighborhoods, those lyrics were now as much a part of those communities as sirens, gun shots and cries.

Richard imagined Rashard's voice being a living thing, creeping through the night, causing all who heard it to stop in their tracks, shiver and bop for a lost one.

Richard was drawn to the sound like a tribesman pulled toward the village drum. It was as if the block had a heartbeat. He crossed 79th and headed toward the lot where the tribe had gathered to praise their fallen witch doctor. The adults from the funeral were outraged.

So disrespectful!
Lost causes!
We living in Chi-raq!
That's why that boy is dead!

Richard wanted to see and to understand. Many

of Rashard's fans were not allowed into the funeral. Since they were locked out, they decided to mourn in their own way. Hundreds of teens pumped to Rashard's track. They lifted up their voices in praise to their hero.

All day! We be grinding all day!

Several cars parked on the east side of the block across from the funeral parlor blasted the same track. Richard felt a surge of energy as he stood amongst the teens. Unlike his experience inside of the funeral parlor, where he was alone in his grief, he felt oneness with this group. They were celebrating Rashard.

He basked in their mutual energy. There was sadness, but it was rimmed in the golden glow of praise and worship. They were draped in white tees, hoodies and sagging jeans. A group in the center of the lot formed a circle around dancers who strutted and juked. They dipped in unison and began to duck walk back and forth. They bopped and beamed and fed off a collective energy not experienced before. One by one each dancer took to the center of the circle to make their offering, each one pushing to a greater light.

Pocket Town players
On the block all day
We bring stunnas on the block all day
Smoking blunts
Stacking paper on the block all day
Until the day we fly away
Living our dreams all day
Dancing on the sun

Laughing down on suckers all day
Living dreams all day
All day—all motherfucking day!

A wave of ecstasy rippled and rose from the left of the lot and swept over Richard and the rest. The harmonic key of Rashard's voice unlocked a door in the spirit of each member of the congregation. Richard could see a kaleidoscope of color glow from the core of each of them. What made Rashard special was within them all. Each congregant moved as one, breathed as one. This family reached back through the portal they had opened to grasp a past unknown to them and with the other hand, reached forward to a future they could not see.

Richard understood. His previous doubts about his path were burned away. In his mind, he saw a new path. His desire to be that director pointing the children in the best ways was clear. The drain of his essence had ended and he was replenished and renewed.

Just then, he heard a voice exclaim "Pocket Town killa!" As heads turned, gunshots rang out.

Pop, pop, pop! Rat-a-tat-tat!

Like a herd of gazelle rushing from the teeth of a raging lion, folks ran from the gunfire. Richard fell toward a young girl who had fallen to the ground.

"Stay down. I got you!" he yelled.

The sound of squealing tires and screams crowded the afternoon air. The lot was littered with shivering bodies. After a moment, with no new shots or threats, each congregant sat up.

The young woman looked at Richard with the eyes of a small child shaken by a thunderstorm. He rolled off of her and sat on the concrete trying to catch his breath. He looked out onto 79th Street as police cars screeched to a halt. Richard felt a pair of arms encircle his mid section. The young woman held him tightly with her face resting against his chest. He swung his arm over her shoulders and returned the embrace. He rocked her and felt her lukewarm tears seeping through his shirt.

Richard hugged her. He rocked and hummed. He wanted her to know that she was protected and that she mattered. Just like her generation, Richard wanted her to know that it would be all right. It wouldn't be easy, but eventually they would lift their own voices in a celestial swoon and their whole generation would rise.

THIS SIDE OF GLORY

Nixon loved the cool moist morning air. Being up every day at five a.m. gave him a perspective of Grand Crossing that most didn't see. The streets were clear and quiet. The gray tinted sky was the same here just like any part of town. The singing birds didn't mind the currency exchanges, payday loan stores, barbecue joints and liquor stores. The sun always rose in the same spot and the hood was graced with all its glory.

Nixon had operated The Good News Stand for fifteen years and he saw the neighborhood go through many transitions within that time. The current state was the most tumultuous. 1991 lay in the shadow of the crack epidemic, Reaganomics and mandatory drug sentencing. Each was a viper that had taken a chunk out of black communities all over the country. But after seeing his own neighborhood decimated, Nixon would tear up in quiet moments to himself. He tried to remain positive so that he could continue to see the

good because he was certain that it was still there.

Sometimes he just had to look a little harder to see it. But once he did, he saw the hard work and honesty, the decency and integrity. It was on the people's faces and written on the sides of buildings and on the stone cold concrete. It was a middle-class neighborhood with brick bungalows and tree-lined streets that seemed to shout in praise every time the wind blew. What Nixon saw was a vision of black America that was desperately trying to manifest.

After the morning papers were delivered, the regulars like Zeke began to come by for their news as Grand Crossing awoke.

"Morning," said the raisin-like man, extending his purplish hand.

"Hey, Zeke," Nixon greeted. "How's the business?"

"Business? You know I been out of business since '83!"

"I meant with you, Zeke. Why we gotta go through this every morning?"

"Shit. Why you keep asking?"

"I know. Maybe after fifteen years I should stop. Just toss you the paper, huh?"

"Ah it's fine. I guess I just ain't never got over them niggas burning down my place."

Zeke used to run the Captain's Table restaurant back in the day. You could get breakfast, lunch and dinner there seven days a week, plus they had the best wings on the South Side. It was also a late night gambling spot. They had pool, poker, craps and even a roulette table. It was all good through the seventies.

With the turn in the community though, things became shady and more violent than ever before. One night, Zeke booted two fools who got caught cheating. There was a struggle when one of the dudes got his skull cracked. The next night The Captain's Tables went up in flames. Zeke cried as his spot burned to the ground. Unfortunately for him, he didn't have insurance and that was that. He took the little money he had saved and opened a laundromat, but it just wasn't the same.

Zeke took in the headline on the front of the paper and slowly shook his head. "Damn shame," he started. "The police busted some drug boys over east. They call it 'cutting the head off the snake.' Nothin' but a bunch of lost boys rotting in the jail if you ask me."

"Yeah, I hear ya. Seems like they just scooping them up and dumping them into the system. Don't really seem to work."

"Definitely ain't working for us. You ever wonder if we can get past all this?"

Nixon nodded and rubbed his chin. "Yeah I do. We gotta be strong in the meantime."

"Pass like a storm huh?"

"Yep. Gonna roll on out to the lake, leaving nothing but sunshine behind."

"I like the way you see things, Nix. All right then," Zeke laughed as he turned and moseyed up

Cottage Grove.

A bit after twelve, the papers got low and Nixon prepared to close up and head over to the church to meet with the deacon board. A thin teenager sauntered just to the left of the stand on the Cottage Grove side. He was dressed in thick, black, baggy jeans and a faded blue hoodie that swallowed him. He posted up with his hand holding a cigarette two inches from his face and a crooked lean. He was a part of the street scene not unlike the fire hydrant or signpost he stood in between. He was frozen like that for two minutes. Nixon didn't take his eyes off him. The ash on the cigarette grew as it burned slow.

Just then, a black Impala pulled up in front of the boy. He broke his pose, placed the cigarette between his lips and leaned into the car. He reached behind him and put his hand in his back pocket. His fingers fished for something. He brought it out his hand smoothly and handed it to the driver.

"Ain't this nothing," Nixon said to himself.

The boy pulled himself from the car and stepped back. He flicked his cigarette to his right and went back to his crooked lean. The car slowly pulled into traffic and headed north on Cottage.

"Say, young man…excuse me, son," Nixon said in his direction. "You in the hood."

Finally, the young man turned and faced the newsstand. Nixon saw his face fully and shook his head. "I know you ain't selling that crap right here, are you? This your last time. Take that mess back over to your block. Better yet, stop selling poison all together."

The young man took a few steps toward the stand and took off his hood, tilted his head and pursed his lips as if he was about to explain something to a child.

"Before you say anything, you got to be new around here."

The young man scrunched his face and let out a "huh?"

"Yeah. I'm Deacon Moncrieff from Greater Mount Zion around the corner on Langley. This here is my stand. And this here is my corner. Everybody from around here know that. Except you obviously. My cousin is the sergeant over at the police station on 71st. Your crew should have told you that. Well, look here… if one more car pull up here, you gonna find out what I'm saying."

"You threatening me, old dude?" The boy asked, reaching inside the pocket of his hoodie.

"Please. Some things gotta be sacred in this neighborhood. You all don't respect the church. But you gonna respect this corner. Now get on from here."

The young man pulled his empty hand from his pocket and relaxed his stance. The fading anger loosened his features and Nixon got a good look at the young man.

"Don't I know you?" he asked.

"Hell naw, you don't know me. I'ma step off this corner though because I don't feel like dealing with no shit."

"Naw, I know you. You ever been over to the church?"

The young man softened his stance. "Yeah, my grandma—she used to take me over there back in the day sometimes."

"What's your name?"

"Blood," he said, as he dipped his head and looked up the street.

"Naw. Your real name."

"Kendrick," he said with a hard sigh.

"Kendrick? You're lil' Kenny? Your grandmother was Dorothy Jenkins, right?"

Kendrick looked back at Nixon, raised his head and jutted out his jaw. "You knew my grandma?"

Nixon beamed. "Young Kendrick! I knew it was you." Nixon leaned out even further from the stand and Kendrick took a step back.

"You remember me? That had to be like seven years ago."

"Yeah. You was a little fella then…you was what...maybe twelve, the last time I saw you?"

"Yeah, about that."

Nixon thought back to when Kendrick was a boy. He had legs as small as straws and a smile that lit up the church. He was his grandmother's special baby. She brought him to Great Mount Zion on 81st and Langley every Wednesday for Bible study and Sunday service. Nixon remembered Kendrick was a dynamo. Every King holiday, he would win the blue ribbon in the oratory contest. One year, he delivered the *"I Have A Dream"* speech with such a passion and conviction that members fell out in the pews and were ready to enact that same fight from the sixties on the scourge that plagued the community in the eighties. Word of the boy's talent reached far and wide. When Harold Washington was inaugurated as Chicago' first black mayor, organizers called on the church and had Kendrick deliver King's *"I've Been to The Mountaintop"* speech. Harold the Great took the boy by the hand and lifted it toward the sky as the masses cheered him as a champion.

"Man, you know you was amazing on the microphone. Folks just knew you would be a preacher one day."

"Yeah, well…"

"We lost track of you when your grandma passed away though. Your momma got back custody, I'm assuming?" Kendrick stiffened and licked his lips but remained silent. "Ya'll must have just moved back over here, huh?"

"You ask a lot of questions."

"Well, I ain't trying to get into your business. But your grandma had a lot of dreams for you and I know dealing wasn't a part of that."

"Fuck you, man."

Nixon flinched and looked at the hardness in Kendrick's face. He saw the broken skin upon his knuckles and the filth under his nails. "How's your Momma?"

Kendrick scoffed, "How you think?" He turned to go.

"Uh, hey. Why don't you come back tomorrow?"

"For what?"

"I got a few pictures from back in the day. Church picnic and stuff like that. Your grandma is in a lot of them. I figured you might like to have them."

Kendrick stopped and thought. "I don't need that. I remember her just fine." And he was gone.

Nixon took a deep breath and exhaled the air over his parted lips. He felt a small rumble in his gut and the hair on his neck stood up. Just as clear as day, he saw his best friend Allen lying in a casket. His skin was chalky brown from all the make-up they put on him. It had happened over forty years ago and Nixon could still see all the details. He remembered staring at Allen laying there, waiting for him to move, to get up and jump back into life. He stared, waiting for a finger to move an inch or an eyelid to twitch, but there was nothing.

Allen had died in the street. He was one of the first to get caught up in the dope game when heroin hit Grand Crossing back in the seventies. Allen was another special one that could have been a leader. Nixon's mind spun and he thought back to the day Allen set out on the wrong path.

The day had been crisp and the new school shoes hurt Nixon's feet. The first day of his sophomore year was thirty minutes from getting started. He loved school and he loved the energy that was given off by all the kids. Even if they didn't know it, they were all full of promise and virtue. It gave them a kind of shimmer. He knew he was different from them in the regard of full appreciation for such an observation. He knew he saw things with his heart, through spiritual eyes that saw the real person that God was in love with.

Nixon stopped and took in the scene and the good vibes he felt from the multitude. He walked right into the mass of hopes, dreams, and anticipation. Afros were everywhere with Black Power picks in them. Girls had on skin tight corduroys and wedge heeled shoes. There was a word that went up in the air but quickly faded—revolution. Nixon heard something about brothers getting it together and finally making moves, because, as they said, 'ain't nobody gon' give us nothing.' He heard all this and it made him proud. His generation had already seen so much.

But Camelot turned out to be a mirage and a King was shot from the sky. Uncle Sam wasn't acting like family and peace had followed love right into the garbage bin, but despite all that, they collectively reached out and embraced 1973 and tried to squeeze as much from it as they could.

Nixon moved through the crowd until he saw his main cat, Allen, and a few of the other fellows from the neighborhood. The boys were huddled around and Allen was talking very fast. His head moved as if it was on a swivel. Nixon came up behind Jimmy Scott and listened in.

"Who's that? Oh, Nixon. Yeah, come in man. I didn't know who you were at first," said Allen as he went back to his presentation. "But yeah fellas, all we have to do is go see Pookie and 'em and get a stash. Take it, sell it and then go back and give them their cut. It's easy money, baby," he said with a devilish grin.

Nixon looked closer and saw the joint in Allen's right hand. Nixon took a deep breath and couldn't believe Allen would get involved in dope dealing. He knew Allen was kind of wild, but nothing like this. His mother warned him to stay away from those Greenwood kids. They were the terror of Grand Crossing. Nixon figured Allen and those boys got a bum rap, but now he wasn't so sure.

"I'm telling you fellas," Allen continued. "This can't lose. Come on, let's go try out the product before the bell rings."

Nixon just looked at him and shook his head. The group dispersed and headed for the side of the building. Nixon reached out and grabbed Allen. "Hey man?"

"Nixon. Let's go smoke this joint, baby," he joked. "Can't start school with a straight face."

"Did I hear you right? You 'bout to start selling for Pookie and 'em?

"Yeah. So?"

"Man, we smoke weed, we don't sell it. That

ain't your bag."

"How you know what my bag is? You spent the whole damn summer trying to force yours on me. You don't even really know me," he glowered.

"That's not true," Nixon said, stammering as he fidgeted with his belt buckle.

"Look man, I know you with that God kick," he said. "You finally started listening to your moms and pops and stopped running up behind me. And that's cool. Do your thing, but don't get in the way of me doing mine." He ripped himself from Nixon's grasp and walked off to begin his descent into no man's land.

Nixon stood and watched his friend walk away. Over the next few years, they would still hang from time to time, but Allen walking away that day to smoke that joint was like walking down a road he would never return from. He became Pookie's star. And when he began selling that heroin, it was only a matter of time. Allen was dead a year later. Gunned down by some fools from Pocket Town who were trying to come up by robbing Pookie's stash house on Evans. It was Allen's day to manage the re-up and he just happened to be on hand when it all went down. One of the few survivors was a young cat who had been pistol whipped. He said Allen went out strong.

"Didn't show no fear either. That's probably why they shot him."

Nixon carried a guilt with him over the years. He felt he could have done more for Allen to save him from the streets. The rumbling in his stomach acted like a signal. He would not make the same mistake again. Kendrick needed to be saved. Nixon felt the entire community and countless lives depended on it.

The next morning, Kendrick slowly opened his eyes. He was so groggy from a night of smoking blunts and downing forties. It was as if he was gazing through cotton gauze. Sleep offered no peace. The dream kept coming back, no matter how much he cursed it. He didn't understand the meaning of it all or who the man was that passed him on that dirt trail every night. At first, he felt it was some kind of punishment for the dope dealing and violence he dwelled in. But it seemed that the more he ran from the revelation, the more upset he found himself. He thought about seeing it out but he was afraid of what might happen. What if his heart gave out? What if he discovered something about himself that was worse than death?

He was certain that something was coming for him. He always knew it would be a price to pay for his lifestyle. No way was he getting away from this without a scratch. He expected death. But if it was to come, then he was determined to let it kick in his door and deal with him.

He sat up on the bed and looked out the window. He rose and went toward the bathroom. He looked in the mirror and barely recognized himself. Thinking back on yesterday when he met the newspaper dude, he remembered the church and how good he felt. Grandma had always said he could find peace there. But things changed so fast.

He doused his face with cold water and thought about the things of his day and if it would be his last. He walked into the front room. Dark streaks of dirt smudged the nappy carpet. It felt rough on the bottoms of his feet. A pile of beer cans sat in the middle of the glass table along with a scatter of dried rib-tip bones. His mother was sprawled across the ripped leather couch with the needle hanging loosely in her fingers. A dried stream of blood ran from a vein in her inner arm. His eyes were blank. He took the needle out of her hand carefully, before covering her in a blanket and slipping out the door.

He found himself on the corner of 83rd and Cottage Grove. He didn't remember wanting to come this way. He was meeting his boy Monty and it was the other way. He saw the newspaper dude hanging out the stand.

"Sup?" he asked simply. Nixon turned with a squint and his face loosened when he realized it was Kendrick.

"Hey now," he smiled. Kendrick took a step toward the stand. "I found those pictures I was telling you about. I went digging in a box and found stuff I hadn't seen in years."

Nixon reached down inside the stand and brought out a stack of slick three-by-ten photos. He placed them on a small ledge connected to the bottom door of the stand. Kendrick stepped closer and there was his grandmother's sweet face. She held a smaller version of him close to her. Their cheeks touched. He felt a landslide in his chest—a great wall falling away that caused his legs to wobble.

"You and your granny was the cutest thing ever. You were always right there at her hip."

Kendrick picked up the photo and stared. That frozen moment came alive inside his mind. He relived the love of that day. He went through the stack slowly. He saw a fresher version of himself. "After granny died. My momma moved us over east by Avenue G."

"That's far."

"Yeah. If we took two steps to the left, we'd end up in the lake. Two steps the other way, we were in Indiana," he said as he rubbed his finger over the sleek surface of a photo. "It was hard after granny passed. Things just stopped making sense," he said as he flipped to the next picture.

It was of he and his mother seated at a picnic table. The sun was bright and gave the picture a golden hue with deep green grass behind them. Kendrick's head was thrown back, all his teeth shown in a huge smile. His mother looked at him like he was a treasure. She was young and pretty. A lock of black hair hung in her eyes.

His mother's name was Gloria. She had fallen for a man that took her to the throne of darkness by way of the main line. She would tap into that vein and ride it nonstop to the devil's door, night in and night out.

"Why don't you take those? You can have them." Nixon said softly.

"You sure?"

"Absolutely. No problem."

Kendrick gathered up the photos, straightened them out and slid the stack in the pocket of his hoodie.

"Kenny…I'm here seven days a week. If I'm not here, I'm over to the church…stop back by."

Kendrick looked confused. "Why?"

"Look. Your people wanted more for you. You know what's up. These streets are death. I've seen so many young men fall down son. I once heard someone say 'no sense fighting the streets because concrete don't crack.' Everyone always loses out here. You smart enough to know that. If things stop making sense again, I'm just saying you got a friend over here."

Suddenly, Kendrick's mood changed. "I ain't got no friends! I was all alone when the shit was deep. You ain't gonna be there for me. When my momma drown in that shit, it's just me. I gotta do what I gotta do and that's all it be about." He turned to leave. "Thanks for the pictures and the memories," he said, throwing the words over his shoulder like a heavy sack. "Take care, man."

He stepped quickly up 83rd Street. Nixon shook his head and began to pray. He lifted up praises to God and asked for the life of Kendrick and all the young men like him that were caught by the concrete of the 'hood like quicksand, sinking slowly. There was so much hopelessness and so many bitter feelings. He prayed for a fresh wind to sweep away lingering debris of bitterness and help a new dawn break forth for them.

"Amen," he whispered.

The farther Kendrick got from the newsstand the darker things became. It was as if the sun refused to penetrate the inner blocks of Grand Crossing. Hooded brothers stood on corners, swaying to the sounds of the asphalt.

As he rounded the corner to his block, he saw a jet black Cadillac SUV. A line of fiends stood in a single file line at the passenger side door. He saw just an arm clad in leather handing out product and receiving money. One fiend would get served and then scurry along as another would step up. Kendrick scanned the block for cops. He had only been in this hood for a short time and was still careful. On Avenue G, open air sales were common. No cops graced the block. As he got closer, he saw it was Moon. They caught eyes and Moon called him over with a tilt of his head.

Moon was the man in Grand Crossing, Avalon and Chatham. He worked for the big boss by the name of Disco T. When Kendrick moved on the block, Moon had sought him out. He said that he had heard from the crew over east that he was a real soldier and that he needed a man like him on his team. Kendrick had a flash of a thought that he would go straight and try to enroll in community college. He figured he could take up refrigeration or electrical engineering, but when Moon handed him a fat roll of bills, that thought evaporated.

"Give me a minute," Moon said, holding up his massive hand and stopping a customer in his tracks. The fiend stepped back and the three behind him grumbled and moaned.

"Say, Blood. What's the happs?"

"Nothing much. I was by the other night for my drop. Looked for you."

"I was with this lil' freak. You know how it be."

"Right." Moon smiled and flashed two gold canine teeth. He had a thick and calloused scar that cut across his neck, maybe three inches long. He had survived a hit a few years back. He thought he was tough enough to not have back up with him. Since then he traveled everywhere with a gladiator named Stone. Stone drove him wherever he went and slept in the SUV in front of Moon's house six days a week.

"Look, I got some work for you." The fiends started to get louder in their complaints.

"Hey Stone, serve them fools up before I have to get out and fuck somebody up," Moon scoffed. Stone got out of the driver seat and the SUV rose two feet, relieved to be free of his three hundred pound frame. Kendrick stepped closer to the window as Stone took care of the customers.

"What's up? Need me to make a run?"

"Naw. I need you to back me up tonight. I gotta deal with some niggas the boss don't like."

Kendrick nodded. "Stone ain't enough?"

"Shit, if one nigga with a gun is good, then two niggas with guns is better," he chuckled.

"I gotcha," Kendrick said, trying to smile. The smile fell from Moon's lips and his face froze in a grimace.

"You put in work over east right? I heard you handled your business a few times." Kendrick nodded grimly. "That's what's up. We'll pick you up tonight at midnight. Be sure to load your shit. You gonna need it."

Kendrick's heart jumped. The blood he spilled over east was a do or die thing. He had to blast his way out of a tight spot and caught an enemy in the throat. The other time was retribution for one of his crew getting blasted during a deal.

"Who are these cats?"

Moon turned and looked at Kendrick and scoffed. "Don't worry about all that. Just come in blasting when I give you the signal. Be a soldier. That's all I need you for. Midnight. Out front."

"Bet," Kendrick said. He turned and walked into the courtyard of the brown castle-like apartment building. His legs were lead, each step heavy enough to break concrete. He remembered feeling whole as a boy; he remembered the few good times. Once, he ran in the park and ate cotton candy. His mother had gotten him a huge red kite. It was made of paper, but it held its own against the stiff wind. The one time he flew it, it got caught in the sun and he did not want it to come down again. When the wind was at its strongest, he simply let the line go and allowed the kit to sail away. Up, up, higher and moving due east. He imagined it making it to the lake front and gliding the wind over open water.

He would sometimes pretend to be that kite, sailing high up in the air, above it all. That memory came to him from time to time in flashes. But nowadays the details were not quite as sharp. He wanted to fly away now.

As he stepped into the apartment, he heard rustling coming from his bedroom. "Kenny! That you?" Her voice strained from a dry throat.

"Yeah."

"Where you been? I ain't got my key," she said, clearing her throat as she stepped into the front room. She was sweating and it had begun to seep through her pink t-shirt.

"What you doing in my room?"

She put her hand on her hip and ran the other over her knotted afro. "Told you I couldn't find my key."

"You gonna make me put a lock on my shit? The reason we over this way is because of your stealing ass," he growled.

"Who you think you talking to?"

"Please. It ain't no different than the way them fools talk to you."

"I'm still your mother—"

"So what? Don't pull that with me!" he screamed. "What did that mean when my own momma stole my product and almost got me killed?"

"Ah, see you being dramatic. You was always sensitive. Sweet little boy," she laughed. "They loved you. Wasn't nobody gonna shoot you over a few packets."

Kendrick shook his head and clapped his hands loudly trying to restrain himself. "So when I showed up with no money and no product what you think they was going to do?"

She stammered and her eyes batted quickly, "Maybe just—I don't know? Look, they let you walk away. It worked out."

"I don't believe you. I don't keep my shit in my room anymore. So stop looking." He turned and went into the kitchen and took the milk jug out of the refrigerator. He poured a tall glass, sat down hard in the vinyl chair and gulped half the glass down. She crossed over and leaned against the kitchen sink facing him. She crossed her arms and looked at him with soft eyes. He stared at the floor. She saw the fluffy milk mustache on his top lip and began to weep.

"You don't get it," he said. "You never have. Granny did the job you were supposed to do. How you think that make me feel? Knowing you ain't no different than the fiends at the door?"

"I'm sorry baby. I did this to you. You was momma's baby and now..." she said, letting her voice trail off.

Kendrick didn't need her to finish the sentence. He was no longer her baby. He was Blood. Every morning in the mirror the hardened face of an enforcer, a murderer, a poisoner of lives stared back at him. He jumped from his seat and slammed the door to his room. He flopped down on the bed and laid in the fading light from outside. Night time lurked.

Around midnight, his phone vibrated. He paused the Xbox, freezing Kobe Bryant in mid-air. It was a text to come downstairs. His body was weighted down into the leather chair. He smashed his eyes closed and spoke silently to himself. With a lurch he stood up. The house was quiet and each step he took, boomed. After tonight he knew that there was no return for him. The dreams his granny had for him had been blown away in the stiff winds of his cold life.

After an eternity he made it down to the black SUV. He stopped. The back window lowered and Moon poked his head out.

"You ready, solider?"

"Kendrick took a deep breath and walked over the passenger side and got into the front seat. Moon's voice rose from behind him as the vehicle pulled off.

"This is an order straight from Disco. He wants them fools smoked. So if you show and prove tonight, he gonna wanna meet you. That's big shit homie."

"Right," Kendrick tried to sound steady. Tupac's voice was low on the stereo and Stone rolled the SUV swiftly down Evans Boulevard. The pale light of the moon cast a ghostly shine over the dark streets.

There was no turning back now.

RIP

I heard something pretty interesting once. It was a saying that went "the very best of a man is illustrated in his words." That's what a famous philosopher dude once said, or at least that's what I heard.

It was at this school lecture, one of those ones where you just file into the assembly hall not knowing what's about to jump off. I was just sitting there. Spitballs and "Your Momma" jokes were flying back and forth like always when this tall, stately-looking, old black dude came out onto the stage and just looked at us. Or maybe it's better to say, he regarded us, 'cause he seemed to be taking mental notes on what we were made of. He was looking deep into us. It was kind of scary 'cause nobody had ever looked at me like that. It was like he locked eyes with me, made a quick check on this list in his head and then moved on to the next kid. I think we all felt it, 'cause them kids who had been cutting up didn't say a word.

Then suddenly, it was silent. Not just quiet, I mean real silence. Like how you know silent is deeper than just plain old quiet. I mean like if it was after nighttime, you would have heard crickets. And then we started looking at him the way he was looking at us. I wondered who he was 'cause I had never seen anybody really like him.

Like I said, he was an old dude, but not all broke down and decrepit like them folks at the retirement center off Cottage and 83rd. Turned out he was a retired judge who stepped off the bench to motivate kids into doing something with themselves. He was tall and his back was straight and his chin stuck out like a ledge of a mountain. He reminded me of an old drawing of Frederick Douglass. All class, muscle and dignity. Every word that crossed his lips had enough juice to cause a stir in folks. He told us his name, but I just called him Old Fred.

So Old Fred stared at us and us at him for like a whole minute. And then when it started to get really creepy, he spoke. And spoke. And spoke for, like, an hour nonstop, about all kinds of things from our heritage as black folk to civil rights, our personal responsibility and our futures. What was so amazing about the whole thing was none of us, I mean none of us, made a sound louder than a sniffle. Not even a cough. No giggles or anything. It was amazing to me.

And then Old Fred hit us with that line I told you about: "the very best of a man is illustrated in his words."

Yeah. That was deep to me, 'cause so many people in our hood be talking crap. Like that's all they do. Another reason it stuck with me, 'cause it reminded me of my father.

But not in a good way.

He would be on the negative end of the statement, 'cause if you lined up his words you'd have a mile of cussing so foul, you'd think he was from some foreign country where they didn't speak no English and he came here and learned the language from listening to Richard Pryor or Eddie Murphy records. I mean, like cussing for no reason. You know how he would do. He would get all bug-eyed and just start winging them out there. He get all excited and turn into some cussing tornado. Just ignorant.

Sometimes when my father would snap on me, calling me all kinds of MF's and F this and F that. And then I would imagine Old Fred and wish he could tell my father all that stuff he told us. Then maybe my dad could be silent like we were silent that day. And maybe that quote would shake my father up and get him to think about his words and how he uses them. But you know what? Thinking about it now, my father would probably cut Old Fred off and then cuss his old butt out like he was some nigger on the block and not a retired judge trying to help somebody do something with themselves. That's kind of sad, you know?

Rip was a trip. I never told you why we called him Rip, did I? Well for all my life, that's all he'd allow me to call him. Not Dad or Pop or anything that let on that he was actually responsible for raising me.

Just Rip.

That was his street name when he banged back in the day. He said they called him Rip, 'cause he was quick to rip a fool off on payday. That always made me sad, to think that my father was that dude. You know, every hood in America got at least one. A lowdown thief so hell bent on causing misery, that he would stick up a working man who slaved all week for a check.

I mean, that working dude could have been getting it rough from his boss and taking all kinds of crap just to support his family. That dude just happen to make the mistake of walking down the wrong block on payday and Rip or whatever they call him in another hood, just up and sticks him.

Whenever my father would brag about them days, I would imagine the face of that hard working dude when he'd have to go home to his family with nothing in his pockets. And since that man is a black dude, you know he all prideful, so he didn't tell his old lady what really happened and how he got stuck up. Then that man would break bad with his lady to cover up the fact he been stuck. He would give her some crap about minding her business and then bringing up the fact that she didn't clean the house right or that the chicken was dry or burnt or something—anything to distract from the fact there ain't no money.

Now that woman, she a sista. So you know she ain't gonna take that stuff. She listens to all his mess and then tell him how full of shit he really is. The man goes crazy because his pride can only take so much. I mean, first he gets robbed by some punk and now his woman is putting him in his place. So to save face, he goes upside her head and then he breaks out. I imagine the apartment is probably real quiet at that point. Then the woman picks herself up off the floor. I see her face when her kids get home from hanging on the stoop. They all loud and crazy and she pissed off. She got a right to be. So who she snap on but them kids? Now they feelings hurt.

And then that lady go beg from her momma, so she can feed them kids she just snapped on, and then her momma be disappointed in her daughter for putting up with a trifling man and his trifling ways. The daughter gets mad all over again, so now her and her momma are into it. All that hurt, bitterness and bad feelings 'cause of some fool named Rip or whatever they call him in another hood. That's my father and it makes me sad to say that.

But out of all the things that make me sad about Rip, and there are a lot of them, nothing makes me sadder than what I saw when I stood at the mouth of this alley one day last week. One and a half blocks up from the corner of 79th and Cottage Grove. The left side with the Chinese restaurant. Yeah, the one with the red sign. That's the one.

I was walking home from this girl's house. I was feeling good—you know what I'm saying? It was a regular day, nothing special. The sun was shining and the pigeons was walking around the sidewalk and people moved from here to there just like they always do. Anyway, I come up on this alley and I just stop 'cause of what I was seeing. Wasn't nothing out of the ordinary about the alley at first, just regular with normal alley activities. Well, at the far end was a garbage truck backing up, getting ready for a dumpster. A little further in was a couple of Mexicans going in and out of this warehouse, loading a van full of clothes on hangers. You know that stuff was going to be sold out of some hustler's trunk later on.

So closer in still was a Chinese busboy out for a smoke, just chilling when another chink comes out and says something in that ping-pang language of theirs. Kind of sounded like he was cussing 'cause he was waving his arms all wild as he was pinging and panging. The busboy just stood there and took the last drag off his cigarette and acted like he wasn't paying the fussing dude no mind. Just regular. Even had the typical rat and bum nosing around the dumpster looking for lunch, except the bum in this alley was Rip. It was definitely him. I'm sure of it. Yeah. I know it was 'cause I stared at him for a real long time.

I actually took a step back and used the corner of the building to block me. I didn't want him to see me. I saw how he shifted through the garbage, looking for God knows what. He had a Jewel's shopping cart full of black garbage bags. I couldn't see what was in them, but then I noticed he stopped shifting and got hold of a Styrofoam container. Like the ones you get at take out joints. He opened it up and it was some old Chinese food. I saw half an egg roll and some chow mein noodles. He closed it and put it in the shopping cart. There was a big clear bag of dandelions in the cart, too.

I think he was going to make him some soup. I remember he said he used to make that all the time when he would run away from whatever foster home he was in back in the day. Dandelion soup and old Chinese food. That's where old Rip turned up after what—like five years?

I remember that bad silk suit he had when I was like ten. It was bone white and he would rock it with some gray gators. Remember that? Man, he would be too clean! To see him all bummy now was too much though. I mean, he had on a dirty old Bears sweater and some filthy pants that looked like a potato sack. I ain't even gonna describe the rest of him.

I felt shame for him. I started to say something to him. I saw me taking him and hugging him. I wouldn't even mention the five years. Nope. I would just take him to my crib and get him clean and fed. No Chinese food either. Chicken wings, maybe. That's what I saw in my mind. But that's not what I did. I just stood there frozen. I tried to make my feet work, but it was like they had a mind of their own, as if they remembered how they would run from our house trying to escape the hollering and the cussing. Wasn't no budging them now.

I tried to call out to him, but my tongue had joined in on the revolt. I guess it remembered all them times I bit it to keep from telling Rip how we really felt and how we were. And my heart wasn't no help either. It had healed just fine over them five years and wasn't trying to get broken up again messing with that fool. So it was just my brain screaming inside my head, but no other parts of me would listen. Then, against my will, my feet turned us around and walked us home. I guess I still got some healing to do. That was a week ago.

I went back to that alley yesterday and looked for him, but no go. I been all over the neighborhood and I couldn't find him. I don't know what I would say or even if the rest of me would go along with us meeting him.

I guess I got to get over it, huh? No matter if he don't want to be called my daddy, he still is. And even if thinking about him makes me sad and brings up all the unhappy stuff from my past, he still my daddy. No matter what. I guess we still got time. He ain't that old. I think he got more years ahead of him than behind. Maybe we can get a new history going. I mean, when I wash that dirt off him, maybe all that he was will come off too. The past just going down the drain in a big soapy swirl. Maybe when I wash his hair, I can wash them bad dreams of the foster homes out of his head. Who knows? Some new clothes and shoes-maybe he would walk different. And if a man is walking right, maybe his talk will turn around too? Maybe Rip won't cuss out everybody and tear everything down like he used to. And maybe he could be all stately and dignified like Old Fred was? Who knows? I'm hungry.

Let's go down to 79th and Cottage Grove and get some of that Chinese food.

Yeah, Chinese sounds good.

ONE BLOOD

Vaughn looked at the blue garbage truck slowly making its way up the street as the collectors trailed behind. Each one working his side of the street, scooping up the black garbage bins like a fisherman uses a net. Karla stood halfway in the house and halfway on the porch. She held Khalil on her hip and a diaper bag on her shoulder. She sucked her teeth and patted her purse, which hung on her free shoulder. She stared at Vaughn's profile and waited. She furrowed up her nose, as the garbage truck got closer to the house.

"I forgot my phone. Here."

Vaughn turned and looked at her. She held Khalil out for him. He paused and then offered alligator arms to receive the baby. Karla let the diaper bag fall to the porch and rolled her eyes as she stomped back into the house.

Vaughn shook his head and walked down the stairs toward the car. He held Khalil away from his body, carrying him like a carelessly stuffed package.

Karla had dressed him like a miniature man. Thick cords, brown construction boots, a brown leather aviator jacket and a White Sox cap. He stood at the driver side door, brought the baby in against his body with one arm. He fished in his pocket for his keys with the other hand.

Quip.

The lock popped and he sat behind the wheel with his son in his lap. Khalil was eighteen months and his eyes were bright and greedy. Everything was new and fascinating to him. Vaughn thought the kid was lucky for that.

When Karla said yes to be his prom date, he felt like his life was on the upswing. High school was coming to an end and he could get busy living without school and stuff. He was set for automotive school and her dreams of college made her special. She was more than just a chick down to smoke and poke. What he didn't realize was that automotive school was still school. He was done after three weeks.

"I'm pregnant." She said those words in a gasp like she was low on air.

Things changed.

He decided to move in with her and her momma. It was better than floating from couch to couch with his homeboys. He and his momma fell out when the new boyfriend moved in two years ago.

Karla gave up college to work at a bullshit customer service gig and got bitter. Now all he wanted was to smoke and poke. But Karla kept serving him a tall glass of reality every morning.

You need a job.
Go back to school.
Selling weed won't get it.
Stay out them streets.
You need to stop playing video games all day.
What example will you be to your son?

He started the car with a vroom. The large engine of the Impala growled. The cool air from the vents caressed his face.

Vaughn looked down on his son. His face would change, chubby and round to muscular and slender. But those eyes would be the same. He had his daddy's eyes. Light brown almonds that stopped folks in their tracks.

"Hey. Hey man."

The baby turned and looked at Vaughn's mouth.

"You going to be a better man than me. You gonna be about your shit."

The baby took his hand and tried to stop the words coming out of Vaughn's mouth. His heart sank. He had no idea how he would make this boy's life any different than his own.

He looked out the driver's side window and the garbage truck blocked his view. The collectors took up the bins as they chatted happily. They reminded Vaughn of two studs enjoying a drink at a lounge.

The huge engine of the truck sounded like an elephant that was having trouble breathing. It moved forward beyond his car and he was able to see the other side of the street.

A dude stood on the corner diagonal from the car. His hoodie was pulled down low over his face. His arms were at his sides and his feet were firmly planted. Vaughn squinted and looked further up the block towards 79th Street. Cars and a bus rushed across his view. He periscoped his head around toward the house and Karla was still not on her way out. His pan continued down at Khalil who had two fingers of his left hand in his mouth. He looked up at Vaughn and then hooted.

Vaughn huffed and then glanced back up to his driver's side view. The dude had stepped into the street. His head was raised and with his left hand he pulled off his hood. Vaughn saw the heavy white bandage over a part of his face and the black eye patch. Vaughn's heart jumped into his throat as the dude pulled a pistol from his belt. Sunlight danced across the nickel-plated 9mm as Vaughn's muscles ceased up and he clamped the baby tight to his body. The world began to move as slow as chilled honey.

Hiim!

The sound of the gun was like a single popcorn kernel exploding in a cast-iron kettle. As silver flashed from the barrel, Vaughn's mind flashed back one week.

The smell of mold and funky weed filled the

basement. The leather sectional was crammed with bodies. There were two blunts. One passing from the left and another from the right. The stud in the middle was the lucky one. He toked on both before sending them back the other way. The only light in the room came from a blue bulb over a wooden coffee table that had a cracked glass panel in the middle. The other light came from a flat screen TV at the other end of the basement.

There were two other dudes besides he and Rick and two females that Vaughn didn't know. Both were bust downs. Not worth a rubber in Vaughn's estimation. But another forty and a blunt and anything was possible. Weeded conversations annoyed Vaughn. He always chose to go inside his head and think.

She gonna flip out when she find out I didn't go in for that interview, he thought to himself. She don't understand don't nobody wanna do that shit.

He hated to be around her. Feeling the judgment in her eyes. He took another drink of his brew. Vaughn sat on the edge of the couch. His friend Rick was next to him. Some trap beat forced its way out of blown speakers. It sounded like an audio oil spill with nothing but bass sitting in the air.

The crib belonged to a tall lanky brother. "Who fucked up my shit?" he exclaimed. "I just got this motherfucker. Who fucked up my shit?" His arms were folded across his chest and he leaned back on his heels. He stood mean mugging the party. One by one, waiting for an answer.

"What, man? Wasn't nobody back there but you and that other nigga who just left. He probably did whatever it was," Vaughn said.

"Fuck you. I don't even know your ass. You and your bitch ass boy," he said, jabbing his finger at Rick.

"Wha—!" Rick said as he sat up.

"Ain't nobody do nothing to your game fool. Chill out."

Dude unfolded his arms and now was on his toes. The two females at the end of the coach slid up and moved along the wall. Vaughn put his head down and giggled into his chest.

The messy bass boomed.

Dude took a step. "You better up some ends on my game, nig—" But before he could take a second step, Vaughn sprung from the coach, jabbed his right arm and smashed the glass bottle against the side of dude's face. The crisp crunch of glass and the dull thud of bone filled the room. The dude stumbled back and dropped to the floor right on his ass. A section of his face near the cheekbone flapped open and hung like a leather tongue on a worn work boot. The girls screamed and ran for the stairs. Dude just sat stunned. Rick pulled Vaughn by the arm to the stairs.

"You fucked him up, man!"

Vaughn opened his mouth to scream, realizing the baby was in the direct line of fire. He tried to loosen his grip and send the baby to the floor but his body would not respond.

Slow as chilled honey.

The driver side glass splintered into a hundred small fissures and imploded. The glass fell like rain. The baby howled. Vaughn finally loosened his grip just a bit and was able to push the baby toward the middle of his lap. When the first bullet hit his chest, his fingers locked and he could not let him go.

He was driven back into the car seat. He bounced back out. The seat belt held him. His blood covered Khalil's head and spread down his brown face like spilled varnish on a wood floor.

Vaughn began to slump to the left. His eyes were wide and locked on dude. He still had the gun raised. His working eye seemed to glow. His lips pulled back from his teeth in a horrible grimace.

Another flash and pop.

So slow.

The chime of the microwave poked at his eardrums. He rolled his eyes as his temples began to throb.

"Why you always cooking shit in the microwave?"

Khalil sat in his high chair with green baby food finger painted over his face. "Whoo," he said, looking back and forth at his parents.

Karla scooped another spoonful. "You lucky

I'm cooking anything," she said flatly.

"Tsk. Lucky? I'm tired of frozen dinners. How come your momma and her nigga eatin' chicken and spaghetti tonight? That shit petty."

Karla held the spoon close to Khalil's mouth and he chomped on it and smacked his lips. "Ahh," he cooed.

"We lucky she even let us stay here. She supposed to feed us too?"

Vaughn got up from the kitchen table and went to the refrigerator and pulled out a clear pitcher of red Kool-Aid. "You better off on Link. Shit."

Karla put the spoon down and turned in her chair toward Vaughn. "Stop working? Just so you can have pizza and chicken everyday?"

Vaughn filled the glass to the brim and placed the pitcher with a corner of liquid left back in the fridge. "That bullshit job ain't getting you nowhere anyway," he said as he took a deep swig of the Kool-Aid.

Karla frowned at his throat bobbing up and down as he gulped. "I must have been out of my damn mind." She turned and picked up the spoon.

"What's that? Out of your mind? When? When you started dealing with me? Shit, how you think I feel?"

"Then leave Vaughn! You just taking up space anyway. We don't need you…" The words hit him like a pile of bricks. She continued to berate him, but he had stopped listening. He completely checked out on we don't need you. A blaze came forth in his guts. Sweat formed around his hairline. He felt this when his momma held her boyfriend's hand and looked at Vaughn like he was a stranger. He felt it when his father turned the corner out of his life.

He dropped the glass sending jagged shards and red Kool-Aid across the floor. He was standing over her. One hand gripped the back of her neck. He threw down three quick punches to the side of her head. She spilled from the chair onto the floor as Khalil erupted.

"Wha—nigga...you crazy! You crazy!!"

He looked down at her with his eyes fluttering. He took in quick shallow breaths and gathered himself. He turned and walked out the back door with Karla and Khalil's screams like hands pushing him out into the night. When he returned a month later, she let him back in. He never saw that look she had when she said yes to be his prom date again.

The second bullet barely missed Khalil. It ripped into the soft pool of flesh under Vaughn's Adam's apple. The force sent Khalil to the floor on the passenger side.

"GOAAH!"

An open hydrant of blood covered the dash and front window.

His head flopped down hard. "Aggh." He saw Khalil lying on his back. Eyes so wide. He looked right at Vaughn. Father and son looked into each other.

Vaughn let his tears go.

     The world was gray and his vision was fuzzy at the edges. He could still hear. He recognized the voices of the garbage men. They called out for help and a scream followed closely behind, high pitched.

     Karla.

     His hearing was sharp. There were birds chattering back and forth, a whoosh of wind, cars motoring on 79th, but the baby...the baby was silent.

     Deeper, he heard his own heart still beating, but slowly. Deeper still, he heard Khalil's small heart beating in contrast to his own. Strong and fast. Both his heart and his son's at the same time. One slower. The other gaining strength. He felt the car move, as the passenger door was pulled open. Karla snatched up the baby and ran.

     He could feel one bullet inside of him. The heat singed his insides. The gray of the world was now fading slowly to white. He felt his body begin to vibrate. Slow at first and then much more violently. He could still hear the two heartbeats. Khalil was fine. The pauses between his own beats were longer and more sustained. The whiteness was now complete and his whole body vibrated until it all just ceased.

BO-PEEP'S JAB

"Loose squares! Loose squares!"

Bo-Peep was in full hustle mode. He had been selling single cigarettes for an hour or so on 79th and Cottage Grove. He ran through his agenda as he palmed change and balled up bills. His head was on a swivel taking in all the movement of the four corners. Traffic stayed thick. Horns blared constantly as jaywalkers moved from the currency exchange to the liquor store to the newsstand and back into the inner blocks of the neighborhood.

A haggard woman with a mop of auburn hair piled high stumbled up to Bo-Peep. Her garnet-colored tank top gripped her plump chest. Her wrinkled brown linen shorts hung loosely over her round hips. She held out a dry and brittle dollar bill.

"What's up, Joann? How them titties hanging, baby?" he asked with a cackle while handing her two Newports.

"Well, you see these big motherfuckers, don't

cha? Shit. It's hot as hell."

"And it's only 11 o'clock. These fools gonna set it off this evening. I can feel it."

"July in Chicago is a mother."

"Always has been. Remember that summer of '79?"

"Hell yeah."

"It was a 102 every day it seemed."

"But that didn't stop us from being out. And sharp as hell, right?" She said as she fanned her hand in front of her face.

"Yes indeed. You had fools swooning at the Tiger Lounge every Friday night."

"That red dress is what would do it."

"That and that brick-house you call a body, sweetie," Bo-Peep said, still staring at her ample bosom as Joann just blushed and covered her broken smile.

She sighed and put a cigarette in her mouth without lighting it. She spoke through one side of her mouth. "Yeah, it sure was hot that summer. Hottest I ever remember." She nodded her head and gave a half salute as she turned and made her way East on 79th.

"Where you on your way?"

"Going to get a half dark, over here," she said, pointing at the Harold's Chicken that already had a line of folks waiting.

Bo-Peep watched her amble across the street. He took out a gray rag from his back pocket and mopped up the sweat from his bald head. He rubbed his bulging gut and sent up his chant once more. "Loose squares! Loose squares!"

As time passed, the change started to bulge the right side pocket of Bo-Peep's worn grey dress pants. He tapped the pocket, making the change sing as he hummed a tune.

A short, thin white man strolled to the bus stop and stood a few feet away. Bo-Peep stopped his tune and looked sideways at the man. With his neat hair and pressed suit, he reminded Bo-Peep of an undercover detective he once ran into back on 63rd and Stewart in Englewood. He squinted his eyes and figured the white man was in his mid-twenties.

Just then, a skinny brother named Johnny stepped out of the currency exchange behind Bo-Peep. "What up, BO? Let me get two."

Bo-Peep shooed Johnny away without taking his eyes off the possible detective. "I'll check you later," he said as he tilted his head toward the white man.

Johnny frowned and quickly made his way up 79th Street. "Goddamn shame. Man can't have shit these days," he said as he walked past the white man. He looked in his direct line of sight and sucked his teeth as he mean mugged him, but the white man paid no attention and Bo-Peep shook his head.

"Say man!" he let out. The white man didn't move. He stood leisurely against the side of the bus shelter with a brown leather satchel slung over his shoulder and one hand stuffed in the pockets of his black slacks. "Hey man! I'm talking to you," Bo-Peep said waving his arm near the man.

"Huh, are you talking to me?"

"Naw, I'm talking to the nigga behind you?"

The white man turned and saw that there was no one behind him and blushed. "Sorry. I have a million things on my mind."

"Oh! Like how you gonna bust my black ass huh? It's bad enough out here, ya'll gotta fuck with a man over some squares too?"

"Squares?"

"Yeah. Going to jail for selling cigarettes is some bull. There's plenty of real crime out here, Mr. Po-Po."

The man tilted his head and looked confused. "Oh, you think I'm a cop?"

"Hell yeah, ain't you?"

The white man chuckled. "No. I'm a teacher."

"A teacher. Look like an undercover to me."

"No. I'm just regular."

"I can't remember the last time I saw 'regular' white folk standing on 79th and Cottage, just because. There ain't no Starbucks or Gap around here, man." The white man smiled and nodded. "If you ain't no cop what the hell you doing around here then?"

The white man caught his breath. "I'm just waiting on my bus."

"Just waiting on a bus, huh? You try and arrest me and I'm going to be pissed."

"They really would put you in jail over selling a

cigarette?"

Bo-Peep shook his head. "Hell yeah. They used to didn't care until them Arabs started complaining."

"Arabs?"

"Yeah. They own all the stores around here. They been breaking up packs of cigarettes for years and selling them for a dollar or two, but then when the black man try and do the same thing and start cutting into their shit, then all of a sudden there's a problem."

The white man nodded. "I gotcha." He strolled over to the curb and took a long look down the block for the bus.

Bo-Peep took a square out of his pack and placed it in his mouth. He flicked his lighter like he was performing a magic trick and inhaled deeply. He looked at the white man, sizing him up and scoffed. "Loose squares!" he called. The rest of the city's daily activities didn't stop so why should he, he thought.

Bo-Peep made two more sales. He noticed the white man taking in the transactions out the corner of his eye like a man seeing a forbidden thing.

"What kind of teacher are you?"

"Oh, um—social studies."

"Figures then."

"What?"

"The way you so fascinated by this native shit. You gonna write a book about the anthropological findings on life in the hood, huh?" Bo-Peep laughed while pulling on his square.

"Nope. I had an interview over at Hirsch.

They're looking for a new teacher for the fall. As soon as the bus comes, I'm back on the red line—"

Bo-Peep cut him off. "Let me guess, up north? I knew it. They got high schools up there. Why come all the way down here? Unless you a crappy teacher, who can't get a job at one of the up north schools?"

"Okay yeah, from up north, but a job is a job. Doesn't matter where it is for me."

"Ha. I guess you got a point. But let me take my black ass up your way and see what happen to me. Cops be all over me. You know it too." The white man sighed and nodded. "You ready to go now? Before you was laid back. Sorry to make you uncomfortable, man. It's just the goddamn truth though. It ain't gonna kill ya."

Just then an old man draped in a wool overcoat and knit hat came around the corner. He stopped and raised his arms as if to signal the world to take notice. Rivers of sweat poured down his face, but he made no attempt to wipe it away. He cleared his throat and took in a deep breath.

"Why the sun shining on me?" he bellowed.

Bo-Peep clinched his eyes and hunched his shoulders. "Ah, here we go," he said. He turned and saw the old bum pace back and forth on the corner. He began to point at passing cars. He kept his right hand high as if he were holding a torch.

In his deep and brassy voice, he continued to belt out his street corner sermon. "God is so good to allow the sun to shine on saints and sinners alike. But how many of us acknowledge that?" he continued.

Bo-Peep shook his head and flicked his lit cigarette at the man. "Go on with that shit, Ambrose. Don't nobody want to hear no goddamn preaching today. It's too fucking hot. Take that down to the aid office. They need some entertainment." The old man stared ice-sickles at Bo-Peep. "I'm not playing, Ambrose," Bo-Peep balled his fist and took a step toward the man. The light turned green and Ambrose sluggishly moved across the street.

He turned, back peddling and pointing at Bo-Peep. "Why does the sun shine on you? Are you worthy of its light?" He waved his hands to illustrate the bombastic ramblings.

"Motherfucker thinks he Paul Robeson or some shit. You need to put that in your book, white boy."

"What book?"

"The one you gonna write on the hood. Come on now, I know you gonna make some money off us. Might as well be a book. You can call that chapter The Wannabes."

"Why that?"

"Because this here hood is full of wannabes or should-have-beens. That fool was an actor in high school. Won all sorts of awards, but the hood do what it do and sucked that dream right from his ass. That fool right there should have been a lawyer, the way he can Jew a fool around on some shit they own outright."

"And what about you?" The white man asked.

"Me? Shit. I was a boxer. Golden gloves. You

couldn't tell me shit."

"Oh, you were that good?"

"Hell yeah. I was knocking niggas out all over the city. I was known for my jab. I could stop a city bus with my right jab. Shit, I was known."

Bo-Peep rose up on his toes and began to bounce, the change in his pocket jingling loudly. "I once knocked a fool out the ropes with just my jab." He flicked his right arm, feigning a punch as he bobbed and weaved. He was as big as a gaggle of cows and his belly shook like a garbage bag full of pudding. But even still, the white man saw a grace beneath the mounds of gristle and old age.

Before long, Bo-Peep's lungs began to scream. He stopped and tried to catch his breath. "Yeah, that was my thing, but it was a long time ago." Bo-Peep looked up the street, eyes misty with memories. He could see the punching bag jerking back, left, right before his eyes. The salty smell of sweat from thirty broad necked Turks flooded his nostrils.

Pap-pap.

The sound of leather on skin pushed the sounds of the corner away. When Bo-Peep walked into the gym he felt like he had come home. The structure made sense to him. His strong-arm bullying was going to pay off and give him the life he saw when he read Ring Magazine. The champs who posed on the covers were gaudy kings, high on life and drunk with hope.

To him, that was the only real currency in the world. Not silver, gold or pussy, but a life reamed in the celestial light of hope. Possessing it made you want to grab life like a fine woman and hold her tight. To not have it, meant you may as well stop breathing.

His heart was full. The glory of that long gone time was live. In the present moment, a cop car drove past with its lights flashing and sirens high. The smile he had on his face melted into a grimace.

No longer seeing the gym, he saw the scene of his arrest in front of Ackerman's Hardware some twenty-five years ago. Flashing blue lights slapping the night, the cuffs slicing into his wrist and the sharp edges of pebbles digging into his bended knees.

"So what we got here?" the officer asked.

"Breaking and entering. We got six of them. Fuckers just backed a truck up to the back door. Popped the locked and started filling up!"

"What? What they go for?"

"That nigger over there was carrying copper pipes and this big nigger here was carrying gallon drums of paint."

"Paint? Get the fuck out of here."

"I shit you not."

The cop leaned down and close to Bo's face and shook his head. "So you about to go down to 26th and California and lounge with them animals over some fucking paint? You 'bout the biggest dummy I've seen in a while. Couldn't you find something better to do with your life?"

That question was worse than any punch Bo-Peep had ever taken. The cops laughed and layed in on him until the paddy wagon arrived.

"So it didn't work out, huh?"

Bo-Peep stepped out of his remembrance and looked at the white man with crossed eyes. "Naw, it didn't work out. What you think, motherfucker? Selling cigarettes on the street was a better option? You think that's the shit my dear old daddy really wanted for me? Just like that hoe over there, you think that's exactly where she wanted to be? You sure you a teacher?"

"Sorry, I didn't mean it like that."

"Yeah, okay. Look here, ain't that your bus coming?"

The teacher turned and saw the bus lumbering up the street. "Yeah," he started as he began to gather his things. "Ummm…take care."

"Right. You too. If you get the job try not to jack them kids heads up too bad." The white man sighed and nodded.

The bus door opened and welcomed him on. Bo-Peep watched as the man found a seat in the belly of the bus. Bo-Peep popped another square in his mouth, ran his tongue around the butt of it and sighed.

He panned his eyes around all four corners, clockwise. There was nothing new to see. He placed his hand in his right pocket and fingered the thin stack of bills. He took in a wisp of air and then lit the cigarette. The tickle of the past was fading. The reality of today was hardening like concrete. He blew out a puffy cloud of smoke and went back to the hustle.

"Loose squares. Come on over here, gal! You know you need a smoke. Loose squares!"

GARGOYLES

The blacktop looked like wet leather. Poochie walked straight ahead through puddles of rain toward the five-story apartment building. Sam followed closely but avoided the water. Poochie stopped in front of a gray door next to a dumpster stuffed with black and brown garbage bags. He bent down and took out a crow bar from his bag.

He placed the flat edge between the door and the frame. He leaned to the left with all his body weight and the old wooden door crunched near the lock and he gently pushed it open.

Even though he was small, Poochie packed power. Growing up he would routinely beat up guys bigger than him."When you're as small as me you gotta kick some ass or you're gonna get your ass kicked on the regular," he would always say.

Poochie stepped into the hall and was devoured by darkness. Sam scanned the alley and then stepped in.

"This goes up to the roof."

"Walk soft. These are the back porches."

They started their climb, as quiet as kittens wearing silk socks. They stepped onto the roof and were met with a swirling wind that tossed garbage and grit into the night sky.

"What you think? Maybe get a couple thousand for this whole haul?"

Poochie shrugged. "Maybe fifteen-hundred. Stone statues ain't going for as much anymore. You been laid up under your lady so long, the market done changed on us."

The two stood comfortably overlooking South Cottage Grove like two men eased up to a bar catching up on old times.

"Shit, if you were lucky enough, you'd have a woman like her and you'd stay up under her, on top of her, on the side of her—anyway you could get it, you know what I'm saying?"

"It's that good, huh?"

"Hell yeah."

"What's her name again?"

"Shawana."

"So ya'll getting out of here, huh? Leaving Chi-town?"

"Yeah. She got people in St. Louis that's gonna help us get set up."

"That's cool. When ya'll leaving?"

"In a week."

"Bet. I'm glad for you, man."

"Thanks Pooch."

"While we working just don't be thinking about her fat ass and fuck up one of these statues."

"Don't be putting your mind on my woman's ass. That's my job. And it hasn't been that long. I still got the touch. That young boy you was working with didn't work out too good, huh?"

"Hell, naw. Nigga kept chipping the faces up. Landlords ain't gonna pay top dollar for no fucked up statues. You remember Old Man Hines? Got the court way building over on Evans?"

"Yeah."

"He had gotten a new spot over east, past Yates and wanted some nice clean pieces. Yuppies moving in over there and he wanted the building looking right. Young boy fucked up so many statues, that old man just straight up told us naw. He ended up going to Home Depot."

"He paid full price?"

"They had a sale that week. Ain't that some shit?"

Sam giggled into his fist.

"Hey, let's get started."

They went to opposite sides of the roof with their hammers and chisels.

Clink!

Sam's hands moved deftly like a fine craftsman. He loosened the stone angel from its perch. The mallet came down again onto the top of the chisel, cutting into the concrete.

Clink!

Sam paused. His eyes followed the growing fissure. The two started selling stolen stone statues and fixtures they stripped from the sides of buildings and selling them on the black market ten years ago. It was a good hustle. Not full time, but it was a way to pad their pockets. They would even do the installation on the customer's end. That was another three hundred bucks. Angels and gargoyles were their top sellers. Once a landlord shorted Poochie on a job. He came back two days after putting the statues up and took them right back down. Did the whole building himself. The landlord stopped by the building the next morning and saw his angels had flown away.

Sam was in the process of removing his fourth statue. He lifted the chisel out of the crack and placed it on the other side of the stone cherub in between the base and the side of the building. Down with the mallet. A short, sharp, controlled strike.

A jagged crack appeared in the mortar. It would only take a few more blows to set it free. On his right side, Poochie worked on springing a miniature gargoyle. Its ash-gray complexion was fading into sea green because of the rain and soot from the city air. Its upturned mouth laughed at unseen pain, the furrow of its brow twisted in delight as its horns stabbed toward heaven.

"How's it coming, Sam?" Poochie asked.

"Cool. This one is ready." Sam put down his tools and placed his hands gently on the angel. One hand stroked the head and the other cradled the bottom. He gave a sharp, counter-clockwise twist. The angel was free.

Sam pulled it up over the edge of the building and into his bosom. He stood up on the rooftop and held it out for Poochie's inspection.

"What you think?" Sam turned the stone angel into the moonlight.

"Good stuff. You still got the touch. Damn shame you leaving the business."

Sam turned up his nose and placed the statue in the oversized black tote bag in the middle of the roof.

"If things ever get tight, then I can just pick it up again."

"I gotcha."

"You ever get a feeling that you want things to be different? Like you need things to be different?"

"Hell yeah. Everyday. But when my stomach get to growling or the landlord starts banging on the door, it snap me right out of it. Different takes time. I gotta do what I know works."

Sam began working on the next angel. Suddenly, he froze like he was a statue. His eyes wide at the sound of the rooftop door rattling. Sam pivoted toward Poochie who had his long, slender index finger to his lips. Poochie edged over to the door, careful not to crunch gravel.

Sam stepped softly and joined Poochie on the opposite side of the door and pressed his body flat against the brick wall.

Sam looked at his watch which read 2:30 a.m. Poochie had jammed a rubber wedge under the door before they started working, but the intruder was determined. They pushed and kicked while cussing under their breath.

Poochie placed his left hand on the door to steady himself as he leaned down and removed the doorstop with his right hand. Sam balled his fists and grimaced as his fingernails bit into his palms.

With a thrust, the intruder burst onto the rooftop. The first thing Sam saw was a large round belly and jingling keys.

It was the building's janitor. He towered over them both. He was husky and broad at the shoulders. He had layers of fat that covered old muscle. Poochie had already brought out the small metal rod he carried. It fit perfectly into his balled fist. Poochie pushed the door closed and waited as Sam held his breath.

"Damn door was stuck again. Hey baby, come on out."

Sam's eyes darted left and right as he rose off the edge of the brick wall. There was a 'Baby'? The janitor had brought some broad up to the roof to get freaky, Sam thought.

The janitor turned to meet 'Baby' and all he saw was Poochie's fist barreling in on him. He tried to scream but the blow, powered with the metal rod, slammed into the man's mouth, jamming his screams down his throat. There was only the clap of flesh against flesh and a crunching sound of shattering teeth and bone. The janitor flopped backward.

Sam swung open the door, ready to grab the chick and caught himself. He looked down and saw that 'Baby' wasn't no chick at all. Cowered in the corner of the stairwell was a small-framed teenaged boy. His bones were delicate and jutted against his thin honeydew skin. Sam just stood over the kid and looked down with his chest heaving. Poochie peeked around Sam as the janitor's coughing and gagging was getting louder.

"Looks like we stopped some homo-action from going down. How old you think he is?" Poochie whispered.

Sam shook his head. Poochie stepped around Sam and knelt before the kid. "Hey man," Poochie started, slapping the kid on the leg. "You didn't see anything, okay?" The kid nodded.

"Well, get up and get the hell outta here," Poochie growled. The kid hopped up and bounded down the stairs taking two steps at a time.

Poochie turned toward Sam with a slanted smile. "Sick bastard. I should bust his damn head for getting ready to do what he was going to do." Poochie went and stood over the janitor who had passed out.

The blood flowed from his mouth like a stream of water down a sewer grate. Sam looked at him in disgust. His top lip was shredded and a chunk hung by a tiny thread of skin. Half the teeth across the top were gone.

"You jacked him up."

"Yeah, well—he jacked up our money. Let's be out." The two crossed over to the black tote and prepared to leave. "You know that's about five hundred dollars we leaving behind, right? I should beat him some more."

Poochie tugged the zipper of the bag, leaving both gargoyles and angels to tumble around in the darkness. He bent to pick up the bag.

"On three. One, two, three." They stood to their feet with a grunt. They wobbled over to the fire escape. The gravel of the roof crunched under their feet. Sam looked over the city. The streets were empty. Off in the distance, he saw a traffic signal flash from red to green.

Carefully, Sam planted his foot on the first step and descended two steps slowly. Poochie lined up and placed his feet on the stairs.

"We probably gonna get about a thousand for this. Now see, I told you it was going to be easy."

"Easy? You had to crack a nigger's skull," Sam rolled his eyes. He couldn't wait to get back home. Shawana's plush body would have the whole bed toasty.

"Yeah, but you didn't even break a sweat."

Poochie smiled at the sound of Sam laughing. Sam looked down for a second to get his bearings as he and Poochie turned the first corner of the fire escape. When he looked up, his heart leapt into his throat and he dropped the bag.

"Hey man. What the fuck?" Poochie whispered.

118

It was the janitor. "Poochie!" Sam screamed. Before he could turn around, the janitor had jumped down the first flight of stairs and wrapped Poochie up in a violent bear hug. The bag tumbled against Sam legs, pinning him in the turn of the escape.

"Get the hell off me!" Poochie screamed as he thrashed around like a catfish caught in a net.

"Motherfuckers!" the janitor bellowed. "Look at me! Look what you did to me!" Immediately, a light in an apartment across the alley went on. Sam pushed the bag of statues off his legs. He climbed toward the two.

"I'ma kill you!"

"Fuck! Sam, this nigger crushing me!"

Sam jumped two steps and grabbed at the janitor's arms, but got kicked right in the stomach. All the air rushed from his body as he crumpled and fell back down the stairs.

"Sam," Poochie croaked.

More lights came on and a dog started barking. The janitor wrenched Poochie over his head as if he were a rag doll. Sam tried to gather himself but his legs were jelly. With a mighty grunt, the janitor thrust Poochie right over the edge of the fire escape. He screamed all the way down. Sam never took his eyes from the janitor. He only blinked when he heard the smack of Poochie's head against the concrete.

"You next, motherfucker!" The janitor lurched forward. Sam reached down, unzipped the bag and plucked out an angel.

He tried to bring it down on the head of the

janitor but he was blocked. An uppercut almost sent Sam over the edge.

"Who gonna fix my damn face?" the janitor yelled as Sam pushed back and brought a knee right to his groin. "Shit!" Sam scrambled down the stairs. "Come here, come here!"

Sam heard the sounds of sirens. He looked over his shoulder, but he didn't see the nightmare coming. He made it to the bottom and ran for the car.

Poochie's body lay like a broken toy solider. His head lay in a deep pool of blood. His arms were twisted and his legs were bent in the opposite direction of the way the Good Lord made them. His eyes were open. The whites had turned red and his pupils were dim.

As Sam neared the car a statue exploded in front of him. He turned back and saw the janitor firing the angels and gargoyles down at him. Sam jumped to his left, just barely dodging an angel. He fished the keys from his pocket and leapt in the car. He started it up and just as he put it in gear, the front hood of the car imploded. Sam ducked and thought a missile had hit him. He gasped deeply and looked up. An angel was impaled deep into the hood.

"Shit. What else can go wrong?" He pushed the pedal to the floor and sped from the alley. He looked in the rear view mirror, half expecting the janitor to be running at him like a bionic man or something.

But there was nothing.

He faced forward with his body numb. As he

drove, the half-in, half-out angel stared at him as if its stone eyes were demanding answers.

Sam didn't know who to call. Somebody, somewhere loved Poochie.

Nope, no calls, he thought to himself. Just get the fuck out of here. Grab Shawana and make that move.

Even without the money from the statues, they had enough to grab that next Megabus and make that move. It had to be first thing in the morning. He didn't want to chance it. He pointed the car south on Cottage Grove and thought about what he would tell her. He drove all the way with the stone angel looking him dead in the face.

GOD'S PRECIOUS LOVE

There was a deep funk that lived in the men's shelter known as God's Precious Love. It would waft from the floorboards and creep around the shelter like a specter. As much as the administrators tried to disinfect the place, the funk always remained. The antiseptic smell from the Pine-Sol only made it worse.

Jonas tried to block out the smell and the symphony of snores, farts and creaking bedsprings. He hated life in a shelter, but it was the only place he and his best friend Jimmy could find. For ten years, the two had lived in Minneapolis, but the stone-cold hand of fate had driven them from there. They had to leave all of their things behind and catch the first thing smoking out of town. They could have picked any place in the nation to land, but being creatures of habit, they came back to the only other home they knew.

Chicago.

When they first got back, they stayed with old

friends and fans that still remembered their music and admired them. But lately their charm had run thin. They weren't able to talk themselves into an old partner's basement for the night. They had long ago seen many of their bridges burned.

Such was the life of a lying dope addict.

The brown bitch had laid claim to Jonas' soul a long time ago. As much as he had tried to fight it, her kiss was too sweet, the dreams that came after she slid that good thing on him were too pure. But invariably, when the high would evaporate, he would be greeted with the smash of reality like a brick to the face. His music career, money and self-respect were all pissed down the drain.

There were times when he would come up from a nod and feel the cool brass of his sax against his fingertips, but none too lately. It took great concentration to will away the ghosts of his past potential. It was easier to just accept what he knew was true and present.

The bright red neon cross that hung on the front of the shelter was lit 24/7 and burned right outside the window of Jonas' bunk. Underneath the cross it read, "God's Precious Love Shelters Men from the Evils of the World." Even though they had been at the shelter for a few weeks, Jonas would stop and stare at the cross and read the saying over and over before Jimmy would call out to him.

Jonas gave up sleep and just stared up at the ceiling. The light of the new day crept over the windowsill and Jonas placed his hand into the spill of primrose light. He wiggled his fingers and thought about how hot it would be later that day.

"Same shit, different day," he whispered and rolled over. He could already feel the hunger rising up from his bowels. It would soon set his flesh aflame and he would do whatever it took to douse it.

As bad as God's Precious Love was, it was like the Ritz-Carlton compared to the other flop houses and transient hotels he and Jimmy had stayed in. It had three large bathrooms on each floor. Each bathroom had seven urinals and seven stalls plus a shower area. In most shelters, there was just one shower area for five hundred people to use. The lines were so long that half the day would be gone before you got a lick of soap on your ass.

He sighed deeply and looked out over the long narrow dorm room and the rows of men in beds. Just then, a long stretch of shadow passed over the wall, twenty feet in front of him. The men of God's Precious Love weren't exactly motivated to get out of bed until they absolutely had to. He lifted his head and looked left to see who had risen so early. After a moment, Jonas recognized the source of the shadow. It was a fool named Lee Otis and he was creeping near Jimmy's bunk.

Lee Otis was nothing but a thieving bastard. Jonas knew that. He rose a bit higher to see what his monkey ass was up to. Jonas sat up slowly and slid from the bunk to the floor. The guy on the bottom bunk stirred. Jonas saw Lee Otis reach down into Jimmy's pants which hung on the post of his bunk.

Jonas took a few quick steps and listened for the squeak of wood he expected. When he heard nothing he kept stepping, hoping Lee Otis wouldn't turn around. Jonas' nostrils flared and his eyes were bulging. The hot sun was now filling the room. A slice of heat was right on his neck and he moved six more steps closer.

Lee Otis slipped his hand into Jimmy's pocket. A tidal wave of boiling water crashed inside of Jonas. Only ten feet now, a few more steps.

Squeak!

Lee Otis turned and stared right at Jonas with eyes bulged. Lee Otis bit his lower lip and eased his hand out of Jimmy's pants. Before Lee Otis could open his mouth, Jonas crossed the distance between them. He spun his body like a top and let his fist fly. The sound of a melon being slapped with a baseball mitt went up in the dorm. Lee Otis' head snapped to the side and he caved like a building during demolition. One dude let out a hoot. Jonas stood over the crumpled body of Lee Otis as the men of God's Precious Love cheered Jonas.

Jimmy sat up quickly. "What's happening?"

"Just get your shit before Forte come up here," Jonas said. Jimmy shook his head.

"Forte? Aw, naw. He already told us if we got one more infraction, he was gone put us out."

"Get your stuff, I said!"

Jimmy put together what had happened when he saw Lee Otis lying on the floor like a baby rocked to sleep. Jimmy got up and grabbed his pants and felt for his wallet.

"I never liked his monkey ass no way," Jimmy said.

Boom!

The metal door that lead to the stairs had been thrown open. Forte was on the scene. He was the program director of the shelter. He was seven feet tall and heavy as a gang of cows. He was also as mean as a Klan meeting at midnight and he loved the sight of blood and the taste of tears.

Thud. Thud.

The sound of his size fourteen boots thudded as he came up the stairs. Suddenly grown men turned into weepy little girls and scattered like mice. They ran for the back stairs jumping over the lump that was Lee Otis.

Jonas felt the floor shaking. And like some old and rusted engine with its gears grinding together, they heard Forte's voice. It sounded like grumbling that was coming straight from the pit of Hell. Those grinding gears ramped up and accelerated until Jonas could make out syllables, then words.

"What the hell's the problem?" Forte let out. "You all acting like loose monkeys again? I got to make y'all behave?" There he stood. Death incarnate. He filled the doorframe with his massive body. His black skin shined like leather from all the Vaseline he put on his face. He stepped into the room and Jimmy swallowed hard.

"Who the hell is this?" Forte bellowed. He used his large sandy brown work boot covered with dark red splotches to roll Lee Otis' body over.

"Somebody done knocked Lee Otis the hell out! It had to be you," he bellowed looking at Jonas.

"How you know I didn't find him like that?" Jonas' voice shook.

"Because you got a time bomb in your head, ready to go off at anytime. You quick to slap a nigger. I know your type. But like I told your monkey ass when you and this bitch of yours got here," he said flicking his thumb at Jimmy, "I'm the king and ain't nobody gonna be knocking nobody out 'round here but me! Put your shoes on, nigger! I'm tired of y'all," Forte said. Jimmy quickly stuffed his feet into his gym shoes.

Forte was the craziest nigger Jonas had ever seen and here he was, helping to run a shelter. Story was, he used to be homeless and the executive director, Mr. Samuels, was scared to put him out. He was taking people's dinners, smashing them across the head with trays and just generally being an asshole. Mr. Samuels finally got the courage to kick his crazy ass out, but Forte just smiled as Samuels hemmed and hawed around. "You know why they kicked me out of juvie hall when I was a youngster?" he asked as Samuels just shook his head slowly. "It's 'cause I burned half of that motherfucker down."

They said Samuels' hairline jumped back a few inches when he heard that. He loved God's Precious Love and he knew Forte was crazy enough to do it. So he just hired him on as a part of the staff and the maniac had been there ever since.

Forte got up on Jonas and looked down into his eyes. Forte's face turned into a mass of wrinkles and creases. His eyebrows pitchforked up and you could see his temples pulsate in and out like accordions. He opened and closed his fists rapidly, making his veins sit up on his arms like pissed off cobras. Jimmy closed his eyes and sent up the best prayer he knew. "Lord have mercy," he whispered.

Forte grabbed each of them by the collar and dragged the grown men to the top of the stairwell as if they were satin dolls.

"Come on now, Forte, don't be like this!" Jimmy let out.

"I was just protecting his stuff! We ain't do nothing!"

Forte held them over the edge of the top stair, and with a laugh that chilled Jonas' bones, he pushed them both down the stairs. They howled and moaned, rolling over one another, head over heels like socks tossed in a dryer. Then with a thundering jolt, they slammed into the concrete floor of the foyer. Good for them there was only one flight of stairs.

Jimmy was just a hump of flesh and Jonas looked like a pile of pick-up sticks. Before they could catch their breath, they were wrenched up and thrown outside.

"Thank God I been taking them anger management classes. Who knows what would've happened to y'all?" Forte laughed. He pulled up his sagging pants and stood right over them and continued. "Rule number two at God's Precious Love is no fighting, no exceptions. The both of you is out. Come 'round the back at five and I'll have Doody set out your shit. And that's five on the dot! Cause at 5:01 you know the vultures gonna pounce all over it." And then he turned his wide-as-State-Street back to them and walked back inside.

Jonas stood slowly and picked Jimmy up. The morning business crowd of downtown Chicago flowed around them, moving quickly so as not to catch whatever disease they thought Jimmy and Jonas had. Jonas dusted himself with his free hand and shook Jimmy with the other.

"Man, are you okay?"

It took Jimmy a few seconds, but he finally spoke. "Are we alive?" he asked bewildered.

"What you think?"

Jimmy panned around. His wide eyes were that of a man who had exited a deep dark cave into a bright and unfriendly sun. "I hope we still alive. I would hate to think your ugly self done followed me into the afterlife," Jimmy said.

"Ha! Me follow you? I'll be going in a different direction than you on that day."

"Mmhumpf! What we gonna do now?"

Jonas didn't know the answer at the time, but they always found a way to make it.

Always.

However, being back in Chicago after so long was giving him doubts. They had grown up on the toughest streets the city had to offer. They had the very essence of the city flowing through their veins. But there seemed to be a different aroma in the air this time around. Almost like a harsher wind.

"So I been thinking—" Jimmy started.

"Oh, Lord," Jonas interrupted. "You know that's dangerous."

"What? I will have you know that it's been my great ideas that have kept us alive all this time."

"Do tell."

"What about that time we had that big score—you remember that? Almost half a brick of that black tar?"

"Right, we both got so sick from that cheap shit that we wanted to die just to stop the pain."

"What about the time we came up on that briefcase full of cash? It was my quick thinking that made that happen."

"Right. We did live high on the hog, until Disco T found out it was us who lifted it from the stash house."

Jimmy stopped for a second and just nodded his head. "Well hell. I guess you right. That cash is what got us out of the Chi in the first place though. Ten years we been gone. I ain't got nothing." He slumped down on the curb with his head buried in his chest. As much trouble as he had gotten the two in, Jonas hated to see his friend down.

"Alright, Einstein. So, what's your big idea?" Jonas asked looking down on Jimmy.

Jimmy immediately lifted his head with a bright smile on his face. "Okay, here it is. Let's jump on the train and head back to 79th Street." The look of pride made him look like a kid. Jonas scrunched his face and shook his head.

Just the thought of 79th Street made his head hurt. 79th Street had been their old stomping grounds. They learned about life and music along the streets of the Grand Crossing neighborhood. Their old music teacher, Mr. Watson, had taught them that loving their horns was like loving a woman. You do it slow and thoughtfully or else she will bite. To go back seemed like torture, like coming face-to-face with the things that tormented them.

"Back south? 79th Street? What if Disco finds out we back? We should have just stayed in Minnesota."

"Sota was too hot. You know that. What I figure is that, it's been a lot of years. He may not even be the man anymore. You know how fast them dope boys be falling off. Here today, gone tomorrow."

Jonas nodded. "Yeah, but Disco wasn't your average dope boy. Don't forget about Daddy J."

Daddy J was a mean old vet of the drug game on the south side. He supplied everything from weed and pills to coke and heroin all the way from Roosevelt down to Blue Island. There were twenty-five square miles of city blocks that he flooded with some of the most potent dope the city had ever known. He was deeply connected to the Italians, some even say going back as far as Al Capone, but Jonas doubted if that was true.

Daddy J had built an empire and ran it until he was blind and senile. That was until he finally left it to his spoiled brat son, Disco T. Jimmy and Jonas had gone to school with Disco and he vowed to hunt them down when he found out it was them who had stolen his seventy-five grand.

"He always was a mean fucker," Jonas said.

"Yeah, remember that time he made Ben's old lady suck on his .45 to prove a point?"

"That's some sick shit to make a man watch."

"All over a few hundred bucks."

"Shit, maybe we shouldn't even be in the city?" Jonas asked.

"Where else we got but Chi-town? The only reason we went to 'Sota was because my uncle was there. I still got family and we were always tight. My cousin Bo-Peep will look out for us. I'm sure he still down on 82nd."

"Bo-Peep, huh?"

"Yessir. You know it's always a good time with ol' Bo," Jimmy laughed.

Jonas rubbed his chin, tilted his head and squinted his left eye. "You know that ain't a bad idea.

Not bad at all." Jimmy stood up victoriously knowing that his place as the idea man of the duo was intact.

"I got five bucks. That's enough to get us on the Dan Ryan."

"You mean the red line," Jonas corrected.

"The red line? See that's what's wrong with Chicago now. Wasn't nothing wrong with what it was called in the first place. Stuff change too much. It confuses things. Let's just get our black asses on the train, whatever it's called."

The two ambled toward the subway entrance. They descended into the cool air of the tunnel. "We been away from the South side for too long. 79th gonna open up and hug us man."

"I feel you on that. 79th and Cottage, here we come."

After the long ride Jimmy and Jonas stood at the four corners of 79th and Cottage Grove. Even at eleven-thirty in the morning on a Wednesday, the activity was thick. Traffic swelled towards the stop lights and floods of folk migrated from one corner to the next, stopping off at the Currency Exchange, the Payless Shoes, the Lee Scott liquor store and the beauty supply. Jimmy smiled broadly and swayed excitedly while Jonas stood motionless.

"It's good to be home. Ten years…too long. I wonder if The Tiger Lounge is still open."

Jonas didn't answer and took in all that the corners had to give. There was a mixture of aromas in the air, old chicken grease from the Harold's and the musty onions from the Polish stand. Booming bass kneaded the atmosphere and shook his rib cage.

"Loose squares!"

"Oh shit! That's Bo-Peep right over there. I know that voice anywhere," Jimmy exclaimed.

Just then horns blared as traffic heading east and west hit an invisible wall. Coming due south was a white hearse followed by a white limo and a parade of cars with orange stickers in the upper right corners of their windshields. When the limo that carried the family passed by, Jonas looked into the back and saw a beautiful honey-complexioned sister, young and sad. Her plump round checks glistened from crying. He knew the look. Not knowing who was to be laid to rest, his heart fell to the pit of his stomach. Death always did that to him. The limo sped up followed by an endless stream of various cars.

"Some things never change," he whispered. Jimmy paid no attention and began to cross to the left. Jonas didn't move for a second. The 'don't walk' orange man of the stoplight began to flash and Jonas' feet let go of the concrete. He followed behind his friend and the doubts about the move back to 79th Street ran through his head like squirrels in an attic. Jonas stepped over a massive crack in the street and wished he was back under the cross of God's Precious Love.

DARCY'S GARDEN

With a warm motherly caress, the sun greeted Darcy Robinson as he stepped outside his front door. He looked across the expanse of green grass and saw his wife, Rebecca, down on all fours in her flower garden. Darcy half-smiled. Her rear-end swung back and forth as she worked the earth. He traced her body and thought about what he wanted to do with the rest of his Saturday morning. He closed his eyes and listened deeply, past the 79th Street bus lumbering toward Cottage Grove Avenue, past the voices calling out for this or that, past the chirping sparrows until he heard her very distinct voice like a tiny bell, whispering to her flowers.

Rebecca's garden was a burst of colors. There were tulips, roses, peonies, birds of paradise and orchids, each of several shades of yellow, red, purple and blue. But her pride and joy was the Stargazer Lilly. Strong yet delicate, the most brilliant orange that eyes had ever seen with its pistils always pointed skyward.

A strong gusting wind rocked the flowerbed and rustled up loose leaves in the street. Darcy lost his smile. Rebecca rose from all fours to her knees. She slowly pivoted until she faced Darcy as the wind picked up strength. Darcy called to her. She reached out to him slowly and carefully as if putting her arm through a circle of broken glass. She stopped suddenly, slumped over and fell sideways onto the grass. Darcy jumped from the porch but he got no further. He stood flat like a flower pressed into a book. A sharp buzzing, like bees in a tin can, filled the air. He clamped his teeth and closed his eyes tight as fists.

"Becca!" he screamed out. A dark cloud, like fizzing bubbles of cola, descended on the garden and began to eat away at each flower. They were consumed in a growing and creeping blight that bubbled on the soft petals, liquefying them.

"Becca!" he screamed again. The cloud covered her, eating at her skin until her flesh pulled apart exposing pink, sinewy muscle. The blight ate at the land, coming toward him. He opened his mouth and screamed but all he heard was the buzzing.

Darkness.

Darcy's eyes fluttered open. His chest rose and fell heavily.

1,2,3…

He gathered himself. It was the same dream he fell into every night since Rebecca had died. He stared at the ceiling and followed the highway of cracks that splintered north, south, east and west. He imagined a map that led somewhere. He wanted to travel those roads away from this room and this house to a new place far away where he could rest without pain.

He sat up in the bed. Lukewarm sweat traveled down his chest. The room looked as if a hurricane had hit with dirty clothes in piles, envelopes, loose papers and empty beer bottles assembled haphazardly across the dresser. Rebecca would have snapped. She demanded her space be clear.

"Clutter clogs the thinking," she would say.

He let himself flop back down on his back. He imagined her fussing at him with every dirty dish. Her voice in his head was better than the lonely hum of the fridge. It had been two weeks since the funeral. His life felt strange and foreign. Her family and what was left of his own had been there for him. But at night, when he laid in bed alone, the absence of Rebecca weighed heavy on his heart. His body was tight as he laid in the bed. He dared not cross the invisible border to Rebecca's side. His breathing was shallow as he remembered a time not long ago.

He came home from his job at the garage, hands caked in dried engine oil with a quake in his chest. He wanted to give her more, but was paralyzed by the thought of how. His mouth went dry whenever he would dare envision himself from up under a car.

He pushed into the house, steeped in shame. As he stepped over the threshold, he was met with the warm and spicy smell of pot roast. Cascading waves of Coltrane's sax washed over him.

"Hey babe," she sang out. Without an explanation, she knew what he felt. She knew his heart. She wrapped him in her arms and with that tiny bell like voice, shushed the shame he felt.

"We got each other, babe. That's all we need. Each other."

Darcy finally rose from the bed and stumbled into the kitchen. He turned on the tap and filled a coffee mug to the brim. He looked out the kitchen window to the garden. A car drove up Evans Avenue and the flowers bent slightly in the breeze. He thought back to that horrible day.

It was a Tuesday. He had gotten off the Cottage Grove bus at 79th Street and crossed over heading east. Bo-Peep the hustle man was in front of the Currency Exchange.

"Loose squares! Loose squares!" he belted out, before he noticed Darcy walking by. "Hey, what's up Darcy?"

"It's all good, Bo-Peep. What's happening?"

"Same old 79th and Cottage Grove shit. Something jumped off up near the train station earlier. Somebody got shot."

"Man, what else is new?"

"Right. Hey, your wife said I could come by and cut down them bushes in the back. I can be over by five tomorrow if that's cool."

"If that's what she said, then it's cool with me. You know she the one take care of that yard, man."

"Yeah. You got a sweet one. You sure she grew up around here? Too sweet for Grand Crossing," he said with a chuckle.

"Born and raised. Went to Hirsch and everything."

"Hard to believe. I just had a chick, born and raised over here, pull a pistol on me. That shit ain't sweet at all."

"Maybe its you, Bo?"

"Yeah. I am a motherfucker."

Darcy chuckled and gave a small wave before he continued walking. "Hey, I'll check you later, man." Darcy moved up 79th past the dollar store, the laundromat and the chicken shack. He turned right on Evans feeling light after a long day at the garage. He had left his cell phone at home and appreciated a day without calls that would pull on him.

Clearing the corner, he saw a mob of people on the block. There was a gray Crown Victoria that blocked the middle of the street and his gait began to slow. As he got closer, it felt like he was walking in thick syrup. His steps became more deliberate and his thighs strained. The faces of the crowd became clearer the closer he got. They were in front of his house and Rebecca's mother was at the head of the pack. She looked directly at him. Her face was pulled down into a mask of pain and anguish. He pushed on and the wails of the mob stabbed at him. Brothers, sisters, aunts and cousins all pulled him into a collective embrace. Their words were a mash of sound that he was unable to decipher. He pushed against their hugs looking for Rebecca.

"Becca! Where's Becca? Becca!" he screamed. Their mouths moved but he couldn't understand. It was as if he was lost in a thick forest and he strained to see past the trees to a horizon far off.

There were two detectives that stood on the curb with sorrow in their eyes. He shook his head. A pair of strong hands grabbed him by the shoulders and pulled him around. The mob steeped back, wails still ringing in the air. It was Rebecca's father. His old body was still strong and shaped like a refrigerator. His face was stone and tears crest in his eyes.

"Becca," he started, choking on tears. "Becca…was shot today. Coming home from work… off the train… it was a stray bullet. She gone, Darcy. She's gone." Finally, he gave in and choked on his sobs. The stone resolution crumbled and he fell to one knee.

Darcy's head tilted up slowly as if pulled by an invisible string. He looked directly into the sun. He felt as if he was being pulled upward. He could no longer feel the hands of the mob tugging at him. His legs were no longer on the ground. A tractor beam pulled him into the sun until he was consumed in a blazing yellow light.

The sound of water rushing from the faucet over

the mountain of dirty dishes brought him back from the memory of that horrible day. He slowly brought the mug to his lips, still staring at the garden. The cool kiss of the water startled him. He looked around the house and sniffed. The garbage overflowed and a funk hung in the air. He turned off the faucet and put down the mug. He started emptying the sink and picked up the dish rag.

Hours later the smell of lemon Pine-Sol seemed to give him strength. He opened the door and marched out toward the garden. He looked down on the rows of flowers. He knew Rebecca would never go two weeks without spending time in the garden. He put down the water-can and knelt before the Star Gazers. Weeds had begun to populate the soil. He dug his fingers into the grayish dirt. It was brittle and scratched his fingers. He picked up the can and watered the soil. It immediately turned pitch black. The ground drank heavily and a crisp breeze danced over his skin and he could have sworn he heard a tiny bell.

After watering the garden, Darcy plunged his hands into the bucket of moist coffee grounds. He scooped up a healthy portion and began to sprinkle them into the garden. He flexed his fingers, mixing the dirt and coffee together.

"Yo, Lil D!" a voice rang out. Darcy's back straightened. He turned and saw a short fireplug of a man with white cotton hair poking from under a dingy brown Kangol hat.

It was his father.

Darcy slowly rose to his feet with a grimace and a grunt.

"You need to stretch before you get down there like that. When you start gardening?"

Darcy rubbed his hands together, grinding the residual dirt into his palms. "It was getting overrun with weeds and clovers. Didn't seem right to have it looking like that."

"I understand. Uh, can I come in?"

Darcy hesitated just a moment. "Mm… yeah. Come on."

He waved his hand and walked over to a white iron patio set. He corkscrewed his lips and shook his head as his father limped into the yard. "You got old."

"Fifty-nine ain't old. I'm young enough to do what I got to do," Big D chuckled.

"And what you got to do?" Darcy said with his eyes fixed to the ground.

"Umm, well…look. I didn't come for nothing. I just heard about your troubles. Figured I should stop by."

Darcy nodded his head. He finally looked at Big D and traced the wrinkles around his eyes. Each line ran into a longer one on his face. When he had seen him last, his face was smoother and the hair was just sprinkled with gray. Now, he looked like a strap of leather left out in the sun too long.

"Where were you?"

"I was in Memphis when I heard."

"The funeral was two weeks ago."

"Your aunt ain't call me until a few days before the home-going. It took me some time to raise money for the ticket. How you holding up, D?"

Darcy shrugged. "You could have called."

"Well… you know I ain't much for the phone. Look son…" he said with a pause. "I'm sorry. It's one thing to have somebody leave you—but to have them taken? I can't even imagine. Whatever you need. I'm here for you."

Darcy looked his father in the face and nodded. "I ain't never heard that from you before—I mean, I ain't never had my wife killed neither, but that's a new one."

"Look. I know ours is a tired story. Ninety-nine out of a hundred black boys got the same thing happening to them. My generation just leaves. I can't explain it. I think it started down south. We find a good thing and then trouble come banging on the door. We up. No trouble…uh-huh. Things get a bit tense and we… well… me—look, D—you get what I'm saying?"

Darcy sat down and nodded towards the empty seat. Big D cautiously sat. "I hear the words, Pop. But I can't say that I understand."

"Well…okay, look, I'm going to be around for a bit. I'm staying with your uncle Bobby until we get tired of one another. Maybe we can keep on talking?"

Darcy just sat and stared out into street. Big D covered Darcy's hand as he laid it on the table with his own. Darcy didn't change his stare. But his steely insides softened like butter under the warmth of his father's touch. His shoulders loosened and he relaxed and sat back into the cushion of the chair.

He slid his hand away from his father and rested it in his lap. They sat looking at the roses laced across the white fence. Every few minutes a car would glide by.

"You know the messed up thing about you leaving?" Darcy asked. "It was that somebody else tried to take your place."

Big D was stone in his chair. He cleared his throat and pulled his voice from deep down in his stomach. "Well, like I was saying—" he started.

"Naw. You don't really get it," Darcy interrupted. "You always thought it was just about you and your thing. But we was like dominoes in your life. You left and she tried to put somebody—I think it was three dudes that first year—in your place. Finally ending up with Donald's old ass. Fucker had to be sixty. He beat her every Friday night. Think on that." Darcy's voice was even and just above a whisper. He scoffed and continued. "After coming in from The Tiger Lounge, he'd set that greasy bag of chicken on the coffee table and march right into the bedroom and tune her up for this or for that. But she chose that nigga and kept him around, even after he started beating on me too. And that's her fault. But I can't help but think that if you were there, well..." Darcy allowed his voice to trail off as another few cars drove past. "I couldn't wait to grow up, ya know. Be big enough to stop that shit. I just wanted to protect her. When I turned 14, I felt like I was ready. I marched right in from school, ready to throw blows. When I got upstairs that son of a bitch was dead in front of the TV. Heart attack."

They sat silently. After a few moments, Big D found the courage to speak. "Would it piss you off if I apologized?"

"No."

Big D drew in a deep breath. "I am so sorry, Darcy. For being weak. For not being there. Please let me be here for you now."

Darcy nodded. "I'm not saying we all good. I obviously got some other stuff to deal with. But...but um...you can stay here when you and Bobby get at it."

Big D chuckled and rubbed his belly. They killed a few beers and talked about Jordan's chances of getting a big league hit before going back to basketball. The sun made its exit and they talked about the missing years as the crickets sang in the background.

The next day, Darcy stepped outside. The air was still and the flowers were like strokes on a canvas. He had not been to work since the funeral. His boss told him to take all the time he needed. He even made sure to pay Darcy the previous Friday.

Darcy stretched and yawned and it sat right in his heart to go back to work. The love he received from family and friends could never replace what his wife had given him, but it did help chase away the darkness. Just then Bo-Peep strolled up the block. He held up his hand and waved.

"Alright now, Darcy. Morning to you."

"Sup, Bo?"

"Flowers looking mighty good this morning. You been taking good care of them. That's a good thing," he said as he leaned over the fence and took a deep pull of the flowers perfumes. "Man, I don't know what we would do without this here garden, Darcy. It's one of the few beautiful things in this neighborhood. Touched by God, you know?" He looked over the garden and then up to Darcy.

"You strong, Darcy."

"Why you say that?"

"Going through what you have...it's enough to eat a man up on the inside. Folks turn to drugs or drinking and never find they way out. These streets is rough, taking the best we got, leaving us with the ugly, ya know?"

"Yeah—yeah I do. Thank you, man."

"Nah, thank you. I look forward to this here. Yessir. I do." Bo-Peep waved again and ambled to the opposite end of the street towards 79th.

Darcy came down the stairs and went to the garden. He sighed deeply as he picked up the can. He placed his fingertips into the cool water. He began to water the lilies, the orchids and the rest of the flowers. He stopped at the stargazer and gently touched its stem. His tears fell upon its petals as the passing 79th Street bus rumbled over the broken concrete.

The editors of Vital Narrative Press sat down with Tony Bowers to discuss On The Nine, his debut collection of short fiction and about what inspires him to create and so much more.

VNP: What was the first story you created for the collection?

TB: That would be "Peppermint & Gunpowder." I started that back in 2006 and worked on it a bit here and there and it turned out to be my first published story, in like 2008.

VNP: That is based on a young boy going against his father. There seems to be a lot of that dynamic in the collection.

TB: Yeah it is. I've said that I'm working on my daddy issues with this project. I think overall that is an important transition for a young man. To not battle his father per se, but to size himself up against his father. What type of man will you be? How will you frame the world and decide what is important to you? That comes from questioning and making certain decisions. In that story and others it is in an extreme form. But I think every young man has to go through the process of butting heads with his father.

VNP: Sort of like a rite of passage?

TB: Yes.

VNP: Is that how you came up with that story's title?

TB: For that one, it is a bit bigger. I really feel that the younger generation finds their voices by countering what the older generation presents. It's natural for a young adult to be a contrarian to a point. Again it is how you define yourself in a world that you didn't create. It's important for the young folk to find their way. We may not like how they go about doing it, with their pants hanging and showing their underwear, it's their way of figuring it out. It's natural. It's a part of growing up, hence the title Rites of Passage.

VNP: Can you talk about your relationship to the neighborhood Grand Crossing?

TB: It's where I spent some pivotal years of my life. I grew up living in numerous addresses up and down 79th Street. It's probably more about The 9 than Grand Crossing. 79th represents the state of black life on Chicago's south side. It can be rough, but at the one end there is beauty. Right where you go to the most eastern spot is the lake and a park and beach. We spent tons of time at Rainbow beach. And you follow it for miles through dozens of other neighborhoods, some good others not so good. I lived in almost all of them. I saw life in some raw terms on 79th Street. 79th Street is real and true and honest. When we left school and somebody asked you were you were going to hang out, you'd say, I'll be on The Nine. 79th Street. You can also use that to mean, that something is true and honest. "Yo, that's on The Nine, for real."

VNP: Was it intentional that characters overlapped stories?

TB: At first it wasn't. I noticed one day when I was taking Darcy's Garden through some changes that Bo-Peep just showed up. I didn't stop him. I let him have free reign and do his thang. When I read it back, it worked. From that point I decided that there should be overlap. 79th and Cottage is a shared place by so many people. Each person has his or her own story to tell. Whether they know one another isn't important. How many times have you walked to your local corner store and passed dozens of people on your way? Each one of those folks has their experiences that are different than yours. The thing you share with them is that time and that place. So, I looked for natural places to have one character cross the boundaries of their own story into another character's story. That fascinates me.

VNP: How so?

TB: Stephen King does that a lot and I think that is so

cool that the hero from Salem's Lot makes a cameo in one of the books from the Gunslinger series. I'm sure I'm going to do more of that. It reminds me of alternative universes or when Marvel would have Daredevil guest star in a Spider Man comic. Two separate worlds coming together. That's a trip.

VNP: It seems that hope is a constant theme in the collection. Speak about that. Why is it so important?

TB: You have to have hope. If not then you are as good as dead. If you are hopeless then life is easy to not care about. You don't care about yourself or the life of your neighbor. I think that's why we have the situation we have in America. Many of our young folk don't see themselves in the world as it is, not really, not authentically. What future do they see for themselves? That not knowing can create sort of a black hole where you can get sucked in. It affects us all. That hopeless kid you may be ready to give up on, can be the one that harms a loved one. We have to help them; we are all in this together.

VNP: Did the current events surrounding black men and police inform you in any way?

TB: Absolutely. How could it not? What's interesting, to me at least, is that I wrote Bo-Peep's Jab back in 2009, what's that 6 years before Eric Garner was murder over possibly selling loose squares? I mean, it wasn't about the cigarettes though.

VNP: What was it about?

TB: About being a black man. About being perceived as a threat just because of his color. The fear that society has for black men is so crippling for everyone. We can't get past it. Until we do, we will be unable to walk into a healthy future.

VNP: How do you feel when you hear the term Chiraq?

TB: You know it throws me off a bit, mainly because it's a national term now. It's how the rest of America and the world sees us. It's so not true as well. That gives a person that doesn't live here the idea that is all Chicago is. A damn war zone. And it's not. In the midst of our issues, we still raise our children and work to help each other. We live with dignity and faith. I love Chicago. Now what's funny is that we Chicagoans have been coming up with gangster type terms for our hoods since forever. Terror Town, Wild 100's, you know. But that's us. It's like when you talk about your cousin or something or a brother and you dogging them, but let somebody outside the family say some shit. Oh, it's on. You ready to fight. Even though the stuff you said is probably ten times worse.

VNP: What other influences made its way to the pages of the collection. What inspired you?

TB: Everything inspires me. Mostly the things I see in real life. I think the main tool a writer should have in his kit is a keen sense of observation. Going back to the idea of hope. I got that from something I peeped back in the day. I was driving home…this was about fifteen years ago. It was a Sunday. I had just left church and I was down about some stuff happening in my life. I was really feeling sorry for myself. I pulled up to the stoplight. Where was I? 79th Street. Figures right? There was this sister who was homeless and looked like she had some other issues going on as well, with her health, maybe some addiction. From the first sight she was having a hard time. But as I sat for the light, she began to smile. Now, not a grin but a deep, broad smile from the bottom of her soul. It was golden, it was one of the most beautiful things I have ever seen. My heart broke right there. All of a sudden as tears were streaming down my face I said that if this sister can be so joyful regardless of her situation than surely I can put my life in proper perspective. She didn't have anything but she had hope, joy and God's peace. That inspiration is in everything that I write. This collection is about the beautiful struggle that life can be. But it's not all one thing or another. In those hard and ugly times you will see the very best of man, eventually. Nature will smile on you. So in that sense we don't have to bow down to our circumstances. We can keep our heads up high because we have hope for a better tomorrow.

VNP: Amen. Thank you.

TB: No problem. Thank you.

ABOUT THE AUTHOR

Tony Bowers is a writer from Chicago, IL.
He has earned a B.A. in Marketing
and a M.F.A. in Creative Writing from
Columbia College - Chicago
as well as a M.A. in Teaching
from National Louis University.